I0517311

Night to Dawn 41

Illustrators:
Marge Simon: pages 23, 38, 65, and 86
Chris Friend: pages 13, 22, 54, and 83
Sandy DeLuca: front and back covers, and pages 3, 8, 36, and 64
Elizabeth Hattie Pierce-Collins: pages 32, 43, 79, and 91
Denny E. Marshall: pages 28, 51, and 87

Night to Dawn No. 41, April, 2022, Copyright 2022 by Barbara Custer. All rights revert to individual author and artist after publication. ISSN # 1542-1430; ISBN: 978-1-937769-74-1
Night to Dawn is a semi-annual publication of fiction, poetry, artwork, articles, and review.
Orders, editorial, and queries: Barbara Custer, P. O. Box 643, Abington, PA 19001
Email: barbaracuster@hotmail.com or ntdsubmissions@gmail.com
PayPal orders: venus1021@juno.com.
Submissions: ntdsubmissions@gmail.com; Web: www.bloodredshadow.com

Pickings and Tidbits

Top of the balloon to you! 😊

The corona apocalypse continues to run strong, with Delta and Omicron variants. Please be careful out there. The COVID vaccines usually work, and breakthrough infections are usually mild. As of this printing, many stores, gyms, and public venues remain open with fewer restrictions. Restaurants change their hours and sometimes close or cut hours due to lack of staffing. I managed a trip to Florida this past fall, and I'll continue to travel, albeit with lots of hand sanitizer and masking.

The characters of *Night to Dawn 41* need a lesson on caution. My mom used to tell me never to get into a car with strangers. Especially in Kempka's "Desire for Warmth," the protag trusted the undead, causing her downfall. An overconfident instructor in Lee Clark Zumpe's "Down Twelvemile Slough" lures his students to a dank swamp where he unearths an ancient religious artifact, and with it, unspeakable horrors. Zumpe has often contributed science fiction tales, like "The Starship Magellan," but he blends his science with dark overtones. Two other NTD stories involve voodoo: Linda Barrett's "Lucy Lochner" and Todd Hanks' "Mama Baoli." The protagonist triumphs well in one but gets their comeuppance in the other. Watch where you're going, cautions Hillary Lyons' "Run." The narrator in her story literally ran into an old friend who isn't quite human.

Marge Simon contributed some delightful poetry, fiction, and art for NTD 41. I enjoyed all her prose/poetry; however, "Blue Sky Somewhere" tugged at my heart. It portrays a vampire who grieves for her humanity. She'd give anything to see the sunlight and blue sky again. Sandy DeLuca also has poetry and art featured in this issue, and there will be more prose/poetry from Sandy in the next *Night to Dawn* issue. She did the front and back covers for this issue, too, along with interior art. Denny E. Marshall, Elizabeth Hattie Pierce, and Chris Friend have also contributed illustrations.

Last year, I released Lyn McConchie's *Another Fire*, and a second, *Some Other Traveller*, will come out in the following weeks. The killer virus in these books makes COVID seem like the common cold. I've just released Margaret L. Carter's eBook, *Doctor Vampire* (Margaret L. Carter Margaret L. Carter (bloodredshadow.com), which will introduce you to Dr. Roger Darvell and his wife, the central characters in her books, *Child of Twilight* and *Dark Changeling*. Carter is a vampire aficionado, and if you love a good vampire tale, you'll want to give her books a read. Her serial story, "Astral Affliction," features a young woman tormented by nightly visions. Spoiler alert: astral projection is involved.

Jon M. Fox's "Noorie" is nonfiction. It details a bona fide haunting at an Indian railway station with pictures included. Ghosts exist, and in real life, they can frighten just as much as their fictional counterparts. Rajeev Bhargava's "Halhogr Egod A.D." takes us on a journey while a couple searches for artifacts from Bigfoot. Denny E. Marshall contributed a shortie, "The Driven," featuring zombies that drive a car. And beware of Christopher Dabrowski's "Faulty Products;" one of them will clean out everything from your veins, including blood.

Along with each story, look for haunting poetry from Lee Clark Zumpe, Marge Simon, Matthew Wilson, Denny E. Marshall, Todd Hanks, and Sandy DeLuca.

In other news, I've contracted with Lyn McConchie to publish her books, *Another Fire* and *Some Other Traveller*. The killer virus in these books makes COVID seem like the common cold. I still use Grammarly, but ProWritingAid ran a sale on premium membership, and I jumped on it. Why, if I'm so happy with Grammarly? Grammarly does a great job, but I've read that if you're editing a fiction work, you may get more benefits by using both programs. I have in mind to use both for my WIP. My progress is slow, and I still find Grammarly great for catching typos. If you are using ProWritingAid, I'd love to hear your take on it.

This winter, I shall hibernate with my balloons. I have three book submissions to review, a book review or two to write, and my WIP. I want to close with a big thank you to all the authors, poets, and illustrators who've sent me their work. And again, I want to thank the readers. I appreciate any attention given to my work.

~ Barbara

Down Twelvemile Slough
by
Lee Clark Zumpe

The reluctant moon crawled along the treetops, timorous and seemingly disconnected. The sweeping black water twisting beneath the gnarled old oaks captured neither moon nor stars in its tide. The dark woods stood exceptionally still in the dusk. The hoots and screeches of all nocturnal creatures had been silenced; the gentle rush of wind had been subdued; the lace of Spanish moss so often found swaying from the tropical hammock had been utterly frozen in time.

Submerged up to his waist in the swift current, Preston L'Heureux felt the mud shift and soften beneath his boots – the riverbed would swallow him whole if he stood in one place too long. He thrust his arms beneath the surface and let his fingers waltz over the sandy bottom. Water swirled around his face as his hands dove beneath a half-sunken log.

His fingers brushed against something in the murky depths, something as unyielding as marble. His very touch seemed to kindle it, and it pulsed with newfound heat against the palm of his hand.

Right where they said it would be…

As he pulled the small object from the water, he hoped he had found more than just an ordinary rock coated with decades of moss and sediment. In the darkness, he scratched at the residue, trying to claw away at the grime obscuring its true face – trying to release it from anonymity.

How could he have doubted them…

Half a mile away, the rest of his company had surely discovered his absence. In their semi-drunken stupor, they might manage to arrange a hasty search party, hoping their concern and efforts would earn them passing grades from Professor L'Heureux. He led twenty of his more advanced students into the dense woods to give them an opportunity to perform fieldwork in a well-excavated Paleo-Indian site.

None of them knew he had ulterior motives.

Preston suspected they would not stray far from the base camp. The depths of the Florida wilderness frightened most of the graduate students. Separated from the constant distraction of modern metropolitan life, the young adults had developed a nagging dread in the backcountry, a trepidation not likely eased by the fact that each of their lifelines to the outside world had been severed shortly after their arrival at the excavation site. L'Heureux could not explain the malfunctioning cellular phones, but promised his students no harm would come to them on their short field trip.

He hoped they would not take his temporary disappearance too seriously. The group would be better off huddling around the campfire, passing around the whisky bottle and conjuring up modern myths and urban legends instead of traditional ghost stories.

Preston waded toward the riverbank and the light of his propane lantern. The darkness of the forest pressed in on all sides, threatening to blot out the meager, flickering lamplight.

Still wiping the last clinging dregs from the surface of the relic, he knelt upon the ground, eager to catch his breath.

The slimy object glistened in the light, its willowy contours and velvety emerald surface released from decades of Stygian murk. The small figurine seemed to shudder in his hands by some deception of the twilight. Its form coalesced beneath Preston's astonished gaze.

He would disclose the mystery; he would enlighten others...

Mesmerized by the paradox of its repellent manner of beauty, the archeologist studied the faintly anthropoid silhouette, wondered at its oblong head, which tapered into a writhing nest of tentacles cascading down over its bloated body. The figure crouched upon an altar inscribed with impenetrable glyphs of ancient origin, the claws of its hind legs clinging to the façade.

"In his house at R'lyeh," Preston mumbled, reluctant to complete the chant, even in English.

They had taught him the mantra, word for word, in their abominable archaic tongue...

Cast into the river by some renegade Louisiana swamp-priest, swallowed by the muddy floor of Twelvemile Slough, this significant religious artifact promised to bring wealth and fame to Preston L'Heureux. His research had finally paid off. Years of investigation into Southern subcultures, fringe religions, and exotic cults had led him to this discovery.

Research alone had not brought him here, though.

The dreams began more than a year earlier. At first, they meant nothing. Comprised of little more than random images of crumbling ziggurats and ruined cities, the nightly visions played out like dull education filmstrips shown to elementary school children, recounting the sad demise of some forgotten civilization.

The voices came later – the disembodied, insistent voices that haunted him each time he drifted away from consciousness.

The sound of muffled voices filtering through the thick darkness of the Florida pine scrub shook Preston from his interlude. Looking up, the professor perceived the bobbing lights of impatient lanterns in the distance. His students had finally left the relative safety of the campfire to search the forest.

Preston carefully wrapped a towel around the statuette and deposited it into his backpack. He stood, retrieved his lantern, and started down a narrow spur trail toward the base camp.

As he hiked the twisting, mile-long trail back to camp, Preston imagined the reception he would receive when he returned to Gainesville. His colleagues at the university would praise him for his exhaustive research. His investigation began by tracking down several obscure articles in scholarly journals. Written by a handful of experts who attended the 1908 American Archeological Society meeting, the dissertations recounted the presentation of John Raymond Legrasse – a man who claimed to have found evidence of cult dating back to prehistoric times.

Preston compared the accounts of Legrasse's infamous idol to descriptions of similar fetishes found in the jungles of Africa, in inundated caves along the coast of France, and in megalithic sites scattered across Scotland. Consulting both Heinrich Niemann's *Andere Götter* and the 1685 *Culto Cattivo* of Raymundus, he identified the existence of a religious sect established before the construction of the pyramids – one that had flourished throughout recorded history, yet had managed to survive virtually unnoticed by society.

Preston cringed and froze as a shrill cry spilled through the darkened forest. In the distance, one of the lanterns swung wildly in the night in a spate of frantic activity. In an instant, it fell into the pitch, utterly extinguished. In the infinite silence that followed, the woodland discarded all its lingering illusory charms and reverted to its primal, rapacious deportment. Shadow folded over shadow, and the night sky pressed down upon the leafy canvas smothering the dark wood and painting it in ominous shades – transforming it into something hauntingly familiar.

The path, they conceded, would be fraught with perils…

Through inquiries and analysis, Preston had determined a few refugees from the fragmented Louisiana sect had been active in the central forests of Florida before the Second World War, but it was the voices in his nightmares that pinpointed the location for him. In vivid, prophetic dreams, he had walked through this forest, waded through the black waters of Twelvemile Slough.

In his visions, Preston had also glimpsed the wild-eyed, fanatical cultists staging blasphemous ritual orgies beneath a lurid moon. He had heard them reciting passages in a forgotten language, uttering incantations to stir misplaced gods, worshipping the ancient idol. He had witnessed the blood of an offering jet into the air and splatter the black-hooded faces of a dozen zealots – and watched as the severed head of the sacrifice tumbled to the forest floor.

Preston – still a good distance away from camp – heard his students' voices growing more frenzied. He cursed himself for leaving them alone, cursed himself for leading them into this excursion under false pretenses. Their lanterns drew closer to the central, blazing beckon of the campfire, and he hoped together they would be safe from whatever horrors he had awakened.

The idol was destined to come into his possession…

Another scream pierced the stifling, unnatural silence of the forest; and another lantern sank into shadow. Preston hesitated, hoping the doused light might reemerge from the gloom, hoping he could return to the base camp and find each of his students alive and healthy. As he lingered, the forest seemed to close in around him, threatened to devour the narrow path that offered the only hope of deliverance. Clinging to his backpack, he began running down the narrowing trail toward the glowing campfire. Sporadic shrieks and howls and moans punctuated the night – and the number of lanterns burning in the darkness decreased steadily, one by one.

They had chosen him to bring about a new era of illumination, to indoctrinate a new generation…

As he approached the base camp, Preston checked his pace. He called out to his students, running down the roll call in his head hesitantly – nervously wavering after each name, hoping for a response. The silence mocked him. Then, from the stillness, he heard a faint whisper stirring like a breeze presaging a late night thunderstorm.

Ph'nglui mglw'nafh Cthulhu R'lyeh wgah'nagl fhtagn.

At first, the voices seemed to emanate from inside his head. He had heard the enigmatic chant in his dreams often enough – he understood the meaning of each word, though he could not comprehend the language from which they had been derived. He shuddered as the proverb echoed through his mind.

Ph'nglui mglw'nafh Cthulhu R'lyeh wgah'nagl fhtagn

As he shambled from the darkness into the light of the blazing fire, Preston realized the voices he heard did not spring from his imagination – not tonight. He saw them now, ringing the fire, waiting for him. Though they wore hoods to conceal their faces, he knew who they were. Of his twenty students, twelve had survived – twelve other dreamers, compelled to stray into these tainted woods by the same forces manipulating him. These twelve new disciples eyed Preston feverishly, confident he had secured the relic that would connect them to the distant past – assured through him they would be initiated into the ancient cult.

To bring about enlightenment…

Preston saw a flash of light, heard a rush of wind, felt a dull pressure against the back of his neck. The night spun riotously and his body went limp, slumping forward toward the fire. In a moment, Preston found himself staring up into the twilight, his head rocking back and forth. Unable to feel anything below his neck – unable to cry out or scream or turn away, he watched one of his students remove the sacred statuette from his backpack. The ancient idol shimmered in the firelight, the writhing shadows making its sinewy muscles ripple, its tentacles squirm, its claws twitch.

Drenched in blood, the disciple lifted the idol toward the lurid moon, igniting a new era.

Preston drowned in a flood of slithering shadows.

The End

Hrothgar by Lee Clark Zumpe

Heorot trembled beneath a foul curse
The subject of which was once put to verse;
Hrothgar sought courage to vanquish his foe
But what caused the blight the text does not show.
Beowulf came, knew what he had to do,
(Heroes aren't known for thinking things through);
With no need for proof, he tracked down the thing,
Butchered poor Grendel, which obliged the king;
And, unfulfilled with the count of one dead,
The hero then lopped off Grendel's mom's head!
Mind you, it turns out that Hrothgar had lied:
It seems not one of his peasants had died.
King Hrothgar was once poor Grendel's best friend
Until one day that all came to an end.
Hrothgar is rarely driven by whim,
But never offend him during a swim.
Poor Grendel had made one crucial mistake:
Grendel was slaughtered for fouling the lake.

8

A Desire for Warmth
by
Hal Kempka

Tonya parked along the road shoulder outside the aging cemetery. Overhead, ominous clouds roiled in the late afternoon sky, ensuring she would have the kind of night she loved, dark, deary, and romantic. Nights like tonight always made her giddy with anticipation.

She turned on the interior light and gazed at her reflection in the rearview mirror. Brownish-red lipstick coated her puckered lips, and violet and indigo strips highlighted her thick black hair. Tonya unlaced and removed her jackboots. She stepped from the car and hurried across the small cemetery's grounds, zigzagging around the aged, crumbling headstones.

Tonya ran toward a large cement and stone crypt nestled against a towering oak tree. The earlier storm had soaked the unkempt grass and earth, and they squished beneath her toes. It resembled a small cottage, though the chunks of crumbled concrete and stone littering the ground near the entrance indicated it had seen better years.

A large rusted lock that had been forced open long ago hung loose on the heavy wooden door. Tonya pulled a knife from her waistband and slowly pushed against the heavy door. It gave with a loud groan, and she stepped inside.

The draft whistling through the iron-barred windows swirled about inside the crypt and swept past her. Its bitter cold stung her cheeks as though she'd been slapped for being an unwanted intruder. Tonya lit several candles and set them around the small enclosure.

She ran her hand along the concrete slab covering the burial vault. Its coldness felt the same as her grandfather's cheek had when she touched it to say goodbye at the funeral. She was nine when he died and had nothing more than memories of occasional visits to him and Grandma.

What she loved most about him was, he always answered her questions without judging and always offered his support to solve whatever problem she was facing at the time.

A few days before his death, Tonya and Grandpa stood on the wide porch watching the sunset. He stepped behind her and gently rested his gnarled, calloused hands, hands that could crack walnuts between his fingers, on her shoulders.

She remembered breathing in the smoky-sweet tobacco aroma emanating from his shirt. It intermingled with the Old Spice scent on his freshly shaven face and always made her feel comfortable and secure.

A pastel sunset disappeared past the thick woods that fenced the western horizon. As they focused on the fading cotton-candy twilight, Tonya tilted her head back and gazed up at him.

"The sky looks so sad, Grandpa."

"I know," he replied. "Earth, like us, dies a little each day. Someday the time will come for humanity to end."

"Is that when the meek will inherit the earth?" Tonya asked.

"No, honey," he replied. "I'm afraid the greedy, vile scum that feeds off people like us will claim it as theirs."

"Why is life so unfair?"

"No one knows. However, if the world of the living is poisoned, the world of the dead will probably be filled with love."

That night, shortly after midnight, he died. Tonya remembered standing with her mother before Grandpa's casket in the funeral home. He appeared to be sleeping peacefully, as though he was napping on the couch.

A wisp of air brushed against her cheek, and she caught the brief aroma of tobacco and Old Spice. She glanced down at him and thought she saw the hint of a smile on his face. She leaned forward and reached to touch his forehead.

Her mother slapped her hand and quickly led Tonya from the viewing room. Once they stepped into the foyer, she grabbed Tonya's shoulders and stared into her eyes.

"Don't ever touch someone after they are dead. They might grab you and drag you into Hell."

Her mother was a bitch who'd leeched off Grandpa all those years. She used him because she was too damn lazy to work or make a life for them.

Tonya pressed her lips together, though she wanted to scream, "No, Mother! It is not me he will drag into Hell."

After her mother retired for the evening, Tonya climbed through her bedroom window and ran the three blocks to the funeral home. She snuck back in and stood at Grandpa's casket talking to him, even though she knew he wouldn't answer.

After several minutes, she wandered from room to room, gazing at those in repose and speaking to them as though she had a connection.

She felt safe in their company and, from then on, snuck into funeral homes and mingled with those awaiting burial or cremation. In all those visits, not one B movie, brain-feasting zombie, or ghoul materialized.

Tonya recalled her first romantic encounter with one of the undead. When she was nineteen, she visited a friend's grave one evening. She sat on the grass and rested her head against the cool granite headstone. She held a one-sided conversation with him and dozed off.

Tonya wasn't sure how long she'd slept, but a sudden chill and musty odor permeating the cemetery air awakened her. Something held her in a firm yet gentle grasp, and she panicked.

She saw nothing in the moonless night but felt a pair of cold, clammy arms enveloping her. Tonya tried to scream, but her vocal cords felt paralyzed. She shuddered and struggled to break free from the chill of his grip.

He clutched her against his rotting form, emitting a quiet whimper that somehow soothed her. The corpse rocked her slowly in his arms and pressed his face into her thick hair as though basking in its flowery scent.

She wanted to push his hands away and escape, but something stirred within her. Tonya silently surrendered to the gentle, relaxing touch.

She awakened at the first light of dawn, lying naked on the dew-drenched grass. Her head rested against the base of the headstone, and her clothes lay neatly folded next to it. Her hands clutched clumps of grass and earth, though the grave appeared to have been otherwise untouched. Tonya quickly dressed and left, certain she'd dreamt it and that nothing occurred.

From that time on, Tonya craved for the touch of the dead. Once or twice a month, she'd sneak into different cemeteries and find an empty crypt. She would enter it and wait. Some nights, she fell asleep and dreamed of a nocturnal encounter, though most nights ended in disappointment

****

Tonya spread a bedsheet across the concrete bier. She stepped from her skirt and removed her water-soaked, ragged mesh stockings. She shivered as she lay naked on a sheet but soon dozed off. A few hours later, a groan coming from the entrance awakened her.

"I'm in here," she called out softly.

In the darkness, she could make out a form shuffling through the door. As it approached the bier, Tonya noticed it was a woman. She looked to be middle-aged and moved with a stilted gait and awkward demeanor as though confused.

She stood before Tonya, gazing at her through milky, opaque eyes. The tart odor of formaldehyde and rot coming off her pale, grayish skin suggested she'd been recently interred

"I have never done this with a woman," Tonya said, knowing it made no difference to her visitor. She almost broke into a giggle when she asked, "Is there anything in particular you would enjoy?"

The corpse's arms hung limp at her side. Her head protruded forward, and Tonya felt sure she would have spoken to her if it not been for her stitched lips.

Tonya led her by the hand to the sheet that covered the concrete slab and whispered, "Why don't we get comfortable?"

The woman slowly disrobed. Even in death, she appeared shapely with broad hips, a small waist, and pottery-gray breasts that, although lifeless, had not yet begun to droop.

Tonya lay down and helped the woman onto the slab. She stroked the woman's face, and she reciprocated by reaching for Tonya as though longing for human touch.

Tonya gathered the woman in her arms and shivered from the cold, clamminess of her skin. The woman held her tight as if trying to soak up her body heat. As the moments passed, the woman's touch became more demanding and aggressive.

Soft moans grew into grunts, and soon she slammed against Tonya with abandon. For the first time in all her encounters with the dead, she felt terrified. She tried to push the woman away and demanded she stop.

The stitches holding the woman's mouth shut ripped apart. Tonya let out a muffled scream as the woman's teeth tore through her skull. Her fingernails gouged at Tonya's lower belly, and her screams rose in tandem with the searing pain of her disembowelment.

The blackness of death flooded her vision, and Tonya caught a tear-filled glimpse of several more corpses stepping into the crypt to join the orgiastic feast. Her final thought was that Grandpa had been right. Alive or dead, the meek would never inherit the earth.

The End

Darkedge by Lee Clark Zumpe

I remember being a blade once,
A promise of victory;
A harvester of death;
The object of a curse
Upon a warrior's breath.

I cut the air at his command,
I shimmered in the sun.
I slept in leathern bed;
And on days of battle
I was bathed in red.

A name I know he gave to me:
I, a brother he trusted,
I, his only real friend;
Darkedge is what he called me
Till he met his tragic end.

With grace I saw years pass by,
My thirst was yet unquenched,
And still my bite was keen;
But the warrior used me little
For he was not what he had been.

When finally, he roused me from my sleep,
Face withered, eyes distant,
He simply wanted to rest;
I wept for the warrior's youth
As I plunged into his breast.

Haiku I by Denny E. Marshall

police visit home
pet parrot kept repeating
"buried in basement"

Astral Affliction
by
Margaret L. Carter

"So Adele thinks she's being haunted?" Fred lounged back in the leather-upholstered chair and took a sip of his after-dinner brandy.

Watching him in the glow of the parlor's gaslight chandelier, Eleanor heard a blend of worry and curiosity in his voice. His lean, handsome face framed by a shock of golden hair—handsome, at least, as far as an older sister could judge—wore a politely quizzical expression.

His fiancée Adele's heavyset, balding father, seated in a matching leather armchair, snorted, literally, as if to reinforce his chosen image as a no-nonsense captain of industry. "Poppycock. She's having nightmares, that's all. Pre-wedding nerves."

Considering the engagement had become official over a month earlier and the nuptials weren't scheduled for almost a year, Eleanor considered that diagnosis unlikely.

"Now, Henry," said the prospective bride's mother, whose prematurely silver hair contrasted with her serenely unlined face, "we must keep an open mind."

"Ghosts in this day and age? This is a new century, a modern era of unprecedented scientific advances."

Uncle Henry's hardly a fit person to talk about the modern era, Eleanor thought. He might have outfitted his factories with the latest "advances," but he refused to install electricity in either of his houses. His wife, Doris, had been lucky he'd at least agreed to piped-in water. He considered Fred's new Daimler motorcar a tool of Satan. For Henry, it counted as a generous concession to entrust his daughter's health to a scandalous person such as a female physician like Eleanor. *Adele asked for me, though, and Aunt Doris backed her up, so he didn't have much choice.*

Not that the couple were technically her aunt and uncle, but addressing them as such was easiest, even though Doris Tolliver was first cousin to Fred and Eleanor's mother. "Spirits aren't necessarily unscientific, Uncle Henry," Eleanor said. "The Society for Psychical Research claims to have uncovered plausible evidence for such phenomena."

Fred put in, "And the doctor who writes the Sherlock Holmes stories believes in them, doesn't he?"

"Speaking of doctors, I suppose you've called in your regular family physician?" Eleanor asked.

Doris, beside her on a settee opposite the two armchairs, turned to face her. "He did examine Adele, but he couldn't find any definite illness. He prescribed one of his tonics, which doesn't seem to make any difference."

Henry snorted still more emphatically. "No wonder. Useless snake oil."

Eleanor agreed with him on that point, at least. "How long has she been unwell? At dinner, she looked … drained."

Fred nodded. "Not like the last time we saw her at all. Even if it isn't a real haunting, she's not herself." A worried frown underscored the tender concern in his voice. As far as

Eleanor could tell, he cherished a deep fondness for his bride-to-be, if not a flaming passion. The family had taken for granted that Fred and Adele would eventually marry since they had played together as children in the garden of this very house, and both of them seemed content with the prospect.

"About three weeks," Doris said. "She started complaining of those visions—or nightmares—losing her appetite, not getting proper sleep. It's happened every single night."

"She ought to go out in the fresh air more," Adele's father said. "Country life seems to have done wonders for Gwendolyn already. She was rather peaked when she arrived."

"How long has she been here?" Eleanor asked. At dinner they'd also seen Gwendolyn, another distant cousin about Fred's age. at dinner, they'd seen Gwendolyn, another distant cousin about Fred's age. She did indeed look radiant with health. She wasn't the type to take advantage of long walks in the country air, though, being more inclined to spend whole days reading in her hosts' otherwise seldom-used library.

Doris replied, "Almost a month. Her parents are traveling in France, sort of a second honeymoon, and we invited her here so she wouldn't have to rattle around in their London townhouse alone with a few servants."

Eleanor thoughtfully twirled her sherry glass in her hands. "Then she hasn't been troubled like Adele?"

Doris shook her head. "It's true that, if anything, she's perked up in the past couple of weeks."

"Obviously, it's all in Adele's mind," Henry said. "She insists she wasn't asleep and really saw—"

Eleanor held up a hand to cut him off. "No, don't tell us. I'd like to hear it fresh from her with no preconceptions. Considering spirits for the sake of argument, though, does this house have any ghost stories attached to it?"

After a thoughtful pause, Doris answered, "I've heard of only one, and of course, it has nothing to do with us." Their country mansion, slightly less than a century old and haphazardly expanded over the decades, had belonged to another family until the Tollivers had bought it after Henry made a fortune from his cotton mills. "In the 1860s, one of the younger sons, Sir Philip, shot himself in the garden after his sweetheart eloped with another man. Supposedly he wanders the grounds at night on the anniversary of his death, which was only a couple of weeks ago, come to think of it. We've never seen him."

Henry waved his hand to brush away the anecdote like a buzzing fly. "Balderdash."

"Even on the remote chance it isn't," Eleanor said, "it doesn't match the circumstances of Adele's alleged visitations. They're indoors and not confined to a single night." She set her glass on the coffee table and stood up. "We should talk to her now if she hasn't gone to bed yet." Although Adele had dragged herself to her suite immediately after dinner, this early, she might still be awake.

Fred finished his brandy and got to his feet also. "We? Not quite the thing for me to join you in her boudoir, is it?"

"Don't be silly, Fred. She's your fiancée, you've known her since she was in pigtails and pinafores, and you've got your big sister for a chaperone." She smacked him lightly on the shoulder. "Let's go."

After bidding their hosts good evening, the two of them headed along the corridor to the staircase. As they approached the open door of the library, Gwendolyn stepped out, a book under her arm. Although almost ethereal-looking, with her fair skin, platinum hair, and willowy figure, she walked with a confident stride. A healthy blush suffused her cheeks as her gaze met theirs. "Oh, I beg your pardon." She took a quick step backward, even though in no danger of bumping into either of them.

"Not at all," Fred mumbled, glancing away from her. "Um—goodnight."

He quickened his pace, forcing Eleanor to walk briskly to keep up. Once they'd ascended the stairs, she glanced over her shoulder to make sure Gwendolyn was out of sight, then asked, "What was that about?"

"Nothing." His face flushed.

She paused and clutched his arm to stop him. "Likely story. You might as well come clean."

"Really, sis, it's nothing important. It's just that this is the first time we've seen her since Uncle Henry and Aunt Doris's Christmas party. Remember that?"

"I could hardly forget since it was less than six months ago. What about it?"

"I danced with Gwendolyn a few times and kissed her under the mistletoe. It was just a bit of fun, but at the moment, she mistook it for more, and it was embarrassing for both of us. That's all." He clamped his mouth shut in a clear refusal to volunteer anything further.

"Very well, I understand, but you can't avoid her forever. Just behave naturally."

"Easy for you to say." They resumed walking. "About Adele's haunting, though. As you said, she looks drained. You don't think it could be a vampire, like in the book by that theater chap?" A nervous laugh suggested he didn't take the idea seriously.

"No, that would be going entirely too far. Vampires belong in stage melodramas. Spirits, at least, have some claim to scientific support."

"According to the Society for Psychical Research?" In a tone of sudden enlightenment, he said, "Maybe we should hold a séance. That's what the scientific fellows would do, isn't it?"

Eleanor laughed. "Let's not get ahead of ourselves. We should hear what Adele has to say before we consider doing anything." More soberly, she added, "Besides, a séance might reinforce her fears and make her even more convinced her ghost—or whatever it's supposed to be—is real."

A couple of minutes later, the labyrinthine corridors added to the original Regency structure brought them to their destination. Eleanor knocked on the closed door of the suite. "Adele? It's Fred and Eleanor. May we come in?"

At a murmured reply, they opened the door and entered the sitting room adjacent to Adele's bedchamber. In an aquamarine dressing gown that complemented her blue eyes and strawberry blonde hair, she reclined on a sofa with a book open on her lap. A breeze wafted the fragrance of climbing roses through a window open to the deepening twilight. At least the Tollivers didn't cling to the outmoded superstition that night air was unhealthful. Sitting up, Adele laid aside the volume, which Eleanor noticed was *The Celtic Twilight*, by the poet Yeats. "Thanks for coming. I'm sorry I had to desert everyone so early."

"Never mind that," Eleanor said. "The important thing is to get your proper rest." Since their last visit, the girl had lost more weight than she could spare, and in the gaslight from the wall sconces, she looked paler than her naturally fair complexion justified.

Fred leaned over his fiancée to give her a chaste kiss on the cheek, after which he sat beside her on the sofa.

A smile quirked Adele's lips. "No need to try to pretend you're not worried, Fred. I know I look a fright."

Eleanor returned the smile. "I certainly wouldn't go that far."

"Well then, Doctor, what's your diagnosis?"

"I can't volunteer one in a split second. May I?" Stepping close enough to feel Adele's forehead, Eleanor peered into her eyes and clasped her wrist to time her pulse. "You don't have a fever. If anything, your skin feels cooler than normal. Your heart rate is normal, and your breathing doesn't sound labored or congested." Her fingernails and the whites of her eyes had no abnormal tint, either, so, in combination with lack of other symptoms, anemia seemed unlikely. "Offhand, I agree with your family physician that you don't seem unwell in any way aside from pallor and weight loss."

Adele sighed. "I just haven't felt like eating much lately."

Eleanor took a seat on the room's other couch. "Since before or after the trouble started?"

"After, when I started feeling so tired all the time. I haven't even worked up the energy to go riding in the past three weeks, and I used to do that every day we were here, weather permitting."

All right, spending too much time inside could account for the pale complexion. "So that's when you began having the visions, about three weeks ago?"

With a shaky laugh, Adele said, "*Visions* is a tactful way of putting it. Mum and Dad think they're nightmares. Either that or I'm going mad."

Fred started babbling protests at the idea. Eleanor cut him short with the calm statement, "There's no question of that. Anybody can tell you're perfectly sane just by watching and listening to you."

"But Mum sat up in my bedroom for two nights. When the … specter appeared, she didn't see anything. So it has to be my imagination."

"Not necessarily. Last All Hallows Eve, out of curiosity, Fred and I had a reading from a supposed clairvoyant at a party."

Her brother nodded. "She didn't seem like a fraud, did she?"

"I'm sure she wasn't, in the sense that she believed in her own powers. Whether they were genuine or not, who knows? But she did say you and I were both sensitives, and such gifts ran in families."

"You mean if Adele can see this phantom or whatever, maybe you or I could?" His brow furrowed. "Then shouldn't Aunt Doris be able to?"

"The alleged gift might skip generations, like red hair. But we're getting ahead of ourselves again," Eleanor added briskly. "We don't have the basic facts yet. Adele, tell us everything you remember about the incidents."

The girl stared into the distance for a moment, then began. "I'd swear I wasn't asleep. Most often, it happened soon after I retired, before I dozed off, but also a few times when I woke up in the middle of the night. Yes, I know I could've dreamed of waking, but it didn't feel like that. Each time, all of a sudden, the room turned as chilly as if I'd left the window open on a December night. I've never felt that in a dream."

When she paused as if waiting for encouragement, Eleanor nodded. "Go on."

"A faintly glowing mass of … something … appeared in the middle of the room. Like a pearly patch of fog. I tried to sit up and get a better look, but I couldn't move." Her voice quavered on the last word. Fred leaned over and squeezed her hand. "The stuff floated toward me, changing from a blob to a definite shape. By the time it got to the edge of the bed, it looked like the silhouette of a person."

"Any definite person?" Eleanor asked.

Adele shook her head. "It just had a blur where the face should've been, all except for the eyes. They looked like a pair of blue lights." She drew a deep breath as if bracing herself for the next part of her story.

"Then what?"

"It touched me here." She pressed a hand to her upper chest, right below the collarbone. "No pain, only something like a light brush of fingertips, but it was icy cold. It felt like every drop of heat was being sucked out of me. I wanted to call for help, but my voice wouldn't work."

"How long did this last?"

"I don't know." Adele frowned and rubbed her brow. "Even if it hadn't been too dark to read the clock on the mantel, I couldn't turn my head to look at it. On a later night, I tried counting and got up almost to three hundred before it stopped."

"Five minutes or less, then," Eleanor said.

"After a while, the … figure … drew back, lost its shape, turned into a patch of mist, and faded away. Within a minute or two, the room warmed up. The first time, I did think I'd been dreaming. Then it kept happening. I dreaded going to sleep, but the thing came every night whether I was asleep or awake."

"Only once on each occasion?"

Adele nodded. "After it's over with for the night, I'm able to sleep, at least."

Fred lifted her hand to his lips. "Don't worry, dear. We'll get rid of whatever this is." He glanced at Eleanor. "Uh … won't we?"

"We'll do our best." Eleanor leaned forward, resting her elbows on her knees. "I do have one idea. Sometimes in the twilight stage between waking and sleep, people find themselves paralyzed. They're fully conscious but unable to move. In this hypnagogic state, they sometimes experience hallucinations accompanied by a sense of pressure and a feeling of panic. It's perfectly normal, certainly not a sign of madness."

Adele perked up. "You think that's happening to me?"

"Possibly. It's not a perfect explanation. Interrupted sleep because of the incidents could account for your chronic fatigue, maybe, but not the poor appetite and cool skin."

"If this paralysis is my problem, why did it start for the first time so recently? And can you cure it?"

Eleanor said with a wry smile, "In answer to both questions, I don't know. First, though, we need to find out whether the phenomenon is sleep paralysis or something objectively real. For that, I'd like to spend part of a night in your room. As we mentioned, if you're suffering paranormal disturbances of some kind, I might be able to see that misty figure even though your mother couldn't."

Adele smiled, her shoulders sagging with obvious relief. "Tonight?"

"Certainly. There's no point in putting it off. We'll go talk to your parents, and I'll come back — when? Shall we say ten o'clock?"

Leaving Adele's suite, the two of them reported to her mother, and they all retired to the parlor again along with Adele's father. Uncle Henry looked first dubious, then distressed as Eleanor explained her tentative ideas about the "hauntings."

"You're saying she might be seeing things, not just having nightmares? Is there something wrong with the child's mind?"

"Not at all. If that's happening, it's a perfectly normal phenomenon some people experience in the moment right before falling asleep or after waking up." Eleanor turned to Adele's mother. "I want to investigate by sitting with her tonight."

"I did that and didn't see anything when she suffered the attack," Doris said.

"I know, but having a second person try can't hurt. And if I don't witness the apparition, we can be pretty sure it's natural, not supernatural."

"Supernatural? Balderdash!" Henry pronounced.

"Maybe." Eleanor managed a smile that she hoped projected confidence. "The proper scientific approach is to test every hypothesis, though."

"See, just as I keep telling you, Henry," Doris said. "We should keep an open mind."

After a final goodnight, Fred and Eleanor headed back to the upper floor. On the way to the chamber he'd been given, he said, "What are you going to do if a ghost does show up? Should you take along a cross or a bulb of garlic just in case?"

She laughed. "You're thinking of vampires again."

He paused at his door, hand on the knob. "But if it's draining her energy, maybe it's a sort of vampire?"

"Experts in the occult claim there is such a thing as a psychic vampire," Eleanor said. "It wouldn't be the kind that crawls out of a grave and flees from a cross, though."

He gave a mock shudder. "Grave-crawling? Sorry I brought it up. Good hunting, sis."

****

An hour later, carrying an electric hand torch and the latest issue of a medical journal, Eleanor marched along the corridor from her bedroom to Adele's chambers. The girl, already in her nightgown, waited at the door of the sitting room. She led the way into the adjacent bedroom. "It's getting so I dread lying down. Not sure what's worse, waiting for it to creep up on me while I'm awake, as it usually does, or being wakened by it in the middle of the night."

Eleanor patted her shoulder. "You don't have to be afraid now. I'll be watching you the whole time. I'll sit over here if that's all right." She gestured at a daybed in an alcove under the open window.

"That's fine." Stifling a yawn, Adele lay down and pulled the sheet up to her chin.

Like armor, Eleanor thought. "Will it disturb you if I read while we're waiting?"

Adele shook her head. Eleanor extinguished the gas lamps in the wall sconces, reclined on the daybed, switched on the torch, and began reading. Floral aromas and the chirping of crickets drifted in on the night breeze. The almost full moon granted her a dim view of Adele's face. The girl closed her eyes at once, as if determined to fall asleep. After a short while, her stiff limbs under the sheet visibly relaxed.

For Eleanor, the time she had no way to measure dragged. Shifting her gaze back and forth between the pages open on her lap and the sleeper in the bed, she caught her eyelids drooping. *I should've brought something more exciting to read than the latest research on blood transfusion.* She had almost decided either Adele's problem was indeed sleep paralysis or nothing at all was going to happen this night, when something did happen.

The pleasantly cool room abruptly turned cold, and a faint glimmer materialized in midair. For the first few seconds, Eleanor thought the pale shimmer that hovered in the middle of the room might be an optical illusion conjured up by visual fatigue. She turned off her light and rubbed her eyes. In full dark, aside from the moon, she could definitely see a human-size clump of pearlescent light whose faint glow brightened as she watched. It spun in a languid circle as it coalesced into a human shape—a female figure. A pair of blue lights glinted where eyes should have been.

It didn't come inside through the door or window. It simply appeared. It rotated away from her and glided toward the bed. Now it looked almost like a solid body outlined by a luminous halo.

One part of her mind observed, *I'm seeing a ghost. Fascinating.* Another part gibbered in terror. Despite her reading in the field of psychical research and the few seances she and Fred had attended, she hadn't seriously believed in occult phenomena. She'd been dabbling in the subject out of mere curiosity. But if an entire supernatural realm existed alongside mundane reality…

Get a grip on yourself! She set aside the magazine and stood up. Could this apparition be a hoax produced by some kind of advanced electrical equipment? Surely not, for such a device would be too bulky to conceal in an ordinary bedroom. If Adele herself hadn't noticed it, a housemaid would have. *Uncle Henry and Aunt Doris wouldn't stand for anything less than a thorough deep-cleaning at least once a week.* Eleanor stifled a hysterical giggle that threatened to bubble up from her throat. *Anyway, who would go to all that trouble and why?*

She strode toward the bed, shivering in the chilled air. The specter loomed over the entranced girl, who lay motionless with her eyes open but blank. When Eleanor got within arm's reach of the tableau, she gritted her teeth and slapped at the figure. Her hand swept through it with a sensation like dipping into icy water. "Get away from her!"

The thing slowly swiveled around to stare at her with its glittering eyes. She choked off a scream at the sight of its face. *Gwendolyn!*

"Get out of here." Hearing her own voice as a tremulous whisper, she forced herself to deliver the next order in a firm tone. "Leave!"

She stepped closer and waved her arms in the specter's face. It floated backward and upward, faded to transparency, and vanished.

Eleanor gulped a breath, swallowed hard, and returned to the bedside. The room was already reverting to its normal temperature. When she touched Adele's arm, the girl's skin felt cool but not chilled. Adele blinked and gazed up at her. "Was the specter really here? And is it gone?"

"Yes to both. You aren't deranged in any way unless it's contagious and we both are." She managed a light tone, and Adele dutifully smiled with her. "If what you reported about the other times holds true, it won't come back tonight." Eleanor hesitated before asking the next question. "Did you see its face?"

"Just a blur, like always." She smothered a yawn. "Will you sit with me a while longer?"

"Of course." Eleanor resumed her place on the daybed. "I'll stay until you fall asleep again." *Why doesn't she recognize the "ghost" as Gwendolyn? Maybe because she's always in a trance of some kind instead of a normal fully awake state?*

While waiting for Adele to doze off, Eleanor pondered the macabre question that next occurred to her. Had Gwendolyn died in the night? She almost rushed to the other girl's room before the obvious answer came to mind. *No, that wouldn't make sense,* she reassured herself. The haunting had started weeks before—around the beginning of Gwendolyn's visit, in fact. *No need to disturb Gwen tonight over something so farfetched. I'll see her in the morning.*

After Adele's breathing quieted to the steady rhythm of sleep, Eleanor tiptoed into the corridor and headed for her brother's room. After knocking on the door and being invited in, she found him sitting up and reading, still dressed. The scent of a cigar he'd recently smoked lingered in the air.

He closed his book and sprang up as she entered. "Well, what happened? Did you see the ghost? I was about to give up and go to bed."

She took a seat in the armchair next to his. "It isn't precisely a ghost, but Adele isn't hallucinating, either."

"I don't know whether to be relieved she's not out of her mind or gobsmacked by the alternative. What do you mean, not a ghost? You did see *something,* then?"

Eleanor summarized the attack and vanishing of the apparition.

Fred sank back into his chair. "What the devil? How is that possible? How can the haunter be Gwen when she's still alive?"

"There are said to be such things as wraiths of the living. Tales of those visions usually connect them with the moment of death or a warning of danger. If they exist at all, though, they could be the astral body temporarily leaving the physical body."

He rubbed a hand over his eyes. "You're losing me, sis. Astral body? The soul?"

"Not quite the same. It's supposedly one portion of the spirit, capable of detaching itself from the rest of the person. Remember what we read about the ancient Egyptians believing the human psyche was divided into several parts? I've heard sober reports from supposedly credible witnesses of astral projection, as well as claims from people who say they can send their consciousness out-of-body that way."

"So you're saying Adele's ill because Gwen's astral body has been doing that psychic vampirism thing? Do I have that straight?"

"That's essentially it," Eleanor said.

He stood up and paced to the window as if reluctant to look her in the eye. "Blast it, why would Gwen try to hurt Adele?"

"That is glaringly obvious. The Christmas party?"

He shook his head. "But that's not like Gwen, even if she were, uh, jealous." Eleanor glimpsed a flush reddening the part of his face she could see. "She isn't the vindictive type."

Eleanor walked over to rest a hand on his shoulder. "I'm not suggesting malice. She may not know she's doing it."

He turned to her with a quizzical frown. "How's that?"

"Recent studies in the functioning of the brain have made it abundantly clear that an unconscious mind exists. Some part of Gwendolyn's psyche may be causing her astral form to leave her body without her being aware of it—maybe in sleep or trance."

"Unconscious mind? I'll take your word for that." He sighed. "So what do we do now?"

"Now, we get some sleep. Tomorrow, we tell Aunt Doris."

"Oh? Not Uncle Henry?" He sounded as dubious of that idea as Eleanor felt.

"How do you think he'd react, even if I could make him understand or believe what's going on? We'll leave it to Aunt Doris to tell him I've diagnosed Adele's illness and am certain I can cure her."

Fred emitted a weary chuckle. "Even if you aren't."

To be continued...

Orbed Lamp by Todd Hanks

Orbed lamp of the heavens,
she seems at once both
pale and bright,
the sister of the night.
She throws a long,
silver shivering line
of reflection across
the black lake.

Waxes and wanes.
Pinpoints of light,
Jupiter and Venus,
are by her side, like
distant cousins.
Ruler of the tides,
the occult her dark side,
over dreams she presides.
An exemplar of love and
death, rebirth and new life.

Siren of the Purple Flames by Marge Simon

She comes when you are ready
to accept that which you wish,
the answer to your last dream,
the one that you ran from
all your days. She comes
in the moments before
waking, before you can
rub the dark away, or turn
off your alarm. She comes
soft robed in purple flames,
sweet as some familiar fantasy
you never could remember,
sings you back to forever sleep
in the coils of her dark hair.

The Starship Magellan
by
Lee Clark Zumpe

"Confirm status quo," Sinisha mumbled, staring absently at a flickering computer monitor as it spray-painted the screen with a jumble of enigmatic data. The lanky Serbian ran bony fingers across the stubble that capped his skull. His eyes lacked any significant animation, and edgy fatigue clouded his face. Waiting for the tinny voice of the ship's computer to respond, the custodian anxiously swayed from side to side.

Sinisha remembered watching a similar monitor back home, waiting to see whether he had been selected to make the long journey to a new planet aboard the colony transport. Like millions of others, he had participated in a lottery to win a spot on the ship. When he learned he would be among the lucky ones, he ran home to tell his family.

Home.

Home, Sinisha guessed, probably ceased to exist long ago.

"Computer confirms status quo."

Sinisha Popic paced the long central corridor deep inside the transport ship Magellan. Alone in the belly of the ship, he had grown used to the silence – if it could be called silence. In some quarters, the vast ship groaned like an old wooden seafaring schooner; in other places, it purred like a slumbering behemoth. The hum of distant engines pulsed through the bones of the speeding giant as it lurched through space.

Sometimes, something unexpected punctuated the silence, startling Sinisha. Every so often, he heard unfamiliar noises echoing through the winding halls, and though he would try to find a source, he always failed. The Magellan hid her secrets well.

One of the largest vessels ever constructed, the Magellan carried a population of several million inside its sleek hull, but it maintained a crew of only one.

Built to carry a cargo of humans away from their decaying home to a new life on a new planet, the ship preserved and defended itself while its freight slept in cryogenic cells. Regulations, however, insisted that one person remain active to perform custodial duties at all times during the mission. Sinisha had the regrettable responsibility of fulfilling that role – at least for the next few hours.

Technically, Sinisha – and any other custodian selected from the millions of sleeping colonists – could function in place of the ship's computers in the event of a crisis to execute any task necessary to ensure the mission's success. Qualified to adjust the navigational systems, repair life support systems, conduct weapons tests, and overhaul the engines, Sinisha and all the custodians who had come before him had learned quickly that none of these chores ever actually had to be completed. The assignment existed only as a backup in case of an emergency, and emergencies did not arise.

As Sinisha rounded a corner, he heard one of those unexpected and inexplicable noises. This time, it came from the lower decks – down in the hold where enormous food replicators promised to provide enough food to feed a thriving colony on a distant planet. Sinisha had never been down to that level. All the custodians pulled their provisions from a different stock as provided by the ship's computer. Frozen in his tracks, he listened intently as the sound throbbed insistently, softly at first – but becoming gradually clearer.

Emergencies do not arise, he reminded himself.

Still, there had been similar situations, historically. More than a few of his predecessors had claimed that they thought someone or something else inhabited the ship.

Some had become utterly obsessed with the idea. A handful seemed to be driven mad by the prospect.

Sinisha knew all of this because he had read the journals of the former custodians. Each custodian served one Earth year, wandering the labyrinth of twisting passageways, trying to find activities to keep themselves occupied. For the most part, time passed excruciatingly slowly on the Magellan. More than a thousand colonists had served as custodians before Sinisha, and he suspected that thousands more would follow before the ship finally reached its destination.

Sinisha's tour of duty had been uneventful. He spent much of it sleeping, but he found that waking sleep could not match the virtual paradise of cryogenic sleep. Nightmares haunted him, and he frequently woke no less weary than he had been before he slept.

And, of course, there were the noises. In the last few days, they seemed to grow more numerous and adamant. Sinisha had begun to wonder if his predecessors had been on to something – if there was, in fact, something else on the ship. Surely, the ship's computers would have detected any intrusion and acted accordingly.

With only hours between him and the numbing tranquility of cryogenic dreams, Sinisha found himself descending into the lower levels of the Magellan, the fluttering beam of a flashlight nibbling at the shadows beneath him.

"Computer, lights."

A network of lights flickered into life, illuminating a gigantic warehouse stocked with thousands of gargantuan food replication units.

Even as the overhead lights banished the thick, syrupy darkness, something scurried across the floor, rattling and scraping and clattering as it sought refuge.

Sinisha saw them immediately. Four figures, humanoid in form, scrambled for cover amidst the aisles of bulky replicators. Sinisha might have spent the balance of the last several hundred years in stasis, but his memory of wars on Earth remained intact. He recognized their armor-plated suits and their plasma rifles instantly.

"Computer," Sinisha cried as he ducked for cover. "Identify intruders!"

"Scanning…" The ship's computer flooded the hold with laser scanners, grasping at every molecule to detect and isolate any trespassers. While Sinisha waited for the response, he searched a nearby passage for an armory, hoping he could find some form of defense if things got ugly. "Levels eighteen through forty-five inspected. No intruders found."

The custodian barked a curse beneath his breath.

Sinisha cautiously made his way back into the warehouse, skirting the outer wall warily. He finally ran across a munitions panel and plucked a laser pistol from its collection. When he felt the warmth of the gun charging beneath his uneasy grasp, he embraced the delicate confidence the weapon provided.

Back home, Sinisha had been forced into analogous situations: He had been compelled to take up arms in defense of his home, his family. Still a boy during the last major European conflict, he had found himself fighting alongside men and women of all ages, fighting to protect himself and his country.

But that was long ago, in a different age, in another place. Sinisha wanted to put that kind of violence behind him…

A burst of hazy green light lit up the perimeter of the warehouse, and sparks rained down over the floor next to Sinisha. He heard the thunderous roar of the plasma rifle an instant later, and he threw himself into flight. Speeding along the outer edge of the warehouse, he guessed at the intruders' position and fired a few warning shots.

He heard one of them growl something, possibly snapping out orders. Sinisha held his breath, cowering in a tiny niche between huge boxes filled with replacement components for the food replication units. The assurance the pistol had offered quickly faded into little more than fleeting bravado, and the custodian found himself wishing he had ignored the sounds entirely.

Sinisha longed to slip back into his cryogenic cell and peel himself from reality.

"Hey…" The voice of one of the intruders trembled. "Stop shooting … we won't fire again."

Sinisha could do little else but trust their word. In moments, he found himself facing the four intruders, their faces masks now lowered. Much to his amazement, the intruders were human.

"We didn't know you were armed … we just wanted to frighten you so you would let us go about our business." The apparent leader of the group rubbed his brow, his face twisted with frustration. He towered over the others as he paced back and forth in front of them. "We hardly ever run into anyone up here – you caught us off guard. We mean you no harm, of course."

"What are you … thieves?"

"*Thieves*?" The accusation had vexed the commander.

"No," a soft, female voice responded. "We came to get supplies." The only woman among the four stepped forward, putting her hand on the commander's shoulder. Her touch seemed to calm him. "We came for food from your replication units. We aren't stealing. We need it to feed our people. We have no other source of food right now. Our planet cannot sustain us all, not until we can fix the damage we have done."

"I don't understand…" Sinisha eyed the four curiously.

"Down below, there are a half a million people – refugees trying to clean up the world we inherited; trying to establish farms, trying to harness the power of biotechnology to raise new herds of cattle. It's a battle we've been waging for a very long time…"

"But we are making progress," the commander added. He smiled, finally, as if he had been confined to a cavern for years and he had just gotten a glimpse at a ray of sunlight. "The inhabitable zones are expanding. We harvested our first crop last year. But it still isn't enough to feed everyone – we still have to depend on your replicators to make up the difference."

"How did you find the Magellan? How did the ship end up here?"

The commander turned to the woman, and she shook her head. An unspoken exchange took place between the two, and both seemed reluctant to answer Sinisha's question.

"The Magellan – well, as you know, it was programmed to transport a colony to another world; from what we could discern from the ship's computers, it never reached that world."

"The Magellan came back to Earth a thousand years ago. She's been in orbit ever since."

Sinisha stumbled a few steps backward until his shoulders pressed against the wall. He slid to the floor as he felt the revelation crash over him. It made sense: Only someone from Earth could gain access to the ship – only someone with human DNA would get by the scanners without tripping the filters. Only someone from Earth could reprogram the computers to make all this possible.

A thousand years had gone by as Earth spun beneath the orbiting Magellan while Sinisha and millions of other colonists slept completely unaware. The dream of a new home shattered, the nightmare of a tainted and derelict Earth now faced the custodian. He imagined the horrors of the harsh world he once called home, cringed at the scope of the task that loomed before humanity.

"Why didn't you…"

"Wake the others?" The woman had anticipated his question. Turning to her, Sinisha knew the answer she would offer, and knew the answer she would not admit. "We have too little food and too little shelter for our own population. Adding millions more into the fold would be suicide, both to us and to the human race."

Sinisha smiled – he knew there was more. He realized his contemporaries had been part of the problem these people had inherited. Returning them to the world they originally poisoned would only ensure renewed hostilities amidst their numbers, in-fighting, wars, and wanton disregard for the environment. Sinisha came from a different age, and he and the millions of others aboard the ship held the wrong kinds of seeds for the new face of Earth.

Sinisha let the laser pistol in his hand slip to the floor. His bones ached, and his head stung with pain. He was tired.

"Is it beautiful … the lands you've reclaimed? Does it look like it did when I was a boy?"

"We think so." The commander offered the custodian a hand. "You're welcome to come see for yourself – you can join us if you wish."

Sinisha considered the generous offer. He missed Earth. He missed his home.

But this planet was not his Earth.

A little while later, Sinisha climbed back into his cryogenic cell and sank beneath the soothing seas of a very, very long night.

The End

Lucy Lochner's Long Night
by
Linda Barrett

Lucy Lochner sat up in bed and stared at the dark shadow underneath her bedroom window. She woke up to face a feeling of intense dread. Something or someone huddled in the shadows.

"Who's there?" she asked the crouched figure, a fearful catch in her voice.

"Who else is there?" the husky male voice questioned her.

An icy chill ran through the petite blonde's spine. Her heart pounded rapidly. "Is this Rick across the street?" she stammered.

"No," the voice said. "I represent him."

Lucy shot upright in her bed. "Leave me alone!" she screamed, drawing up the sheets to her chin.

Reaching for the lamp on her nightstand, she flicked on the light. In the well-lit room, she found herself staring at the white walls under her bedroom window. The shadow disappeared. Still trembling, Lucy reached for her phone. She pressed the buttons and waited for someone to answer.

She sighed with relief as she heard Agnes Della Rossa's sighed greeting.

"What is it?" Agnes, her former therapist, asked.

"There was someone in the bedroom watching me. It's Rick from across the street. He's been giving me the eye all week long. He practices voodoo, and he put a small coffin with my name on it under the stoop of my front door."

"Lucy," Agnes sighed. "We discussed this before. No one is out to get you. You always call me up and tell me that. Talk to your new therapist. It's midnight. Take your medicine. Good night." Agnes hung up.

Lucy put her phone down and got out of bed. She hurried to the kitchen. The room was pitch-dark. A shadow buried the refrigerator. It moved towards her. She leapt backward.

"Who is it?" she shouted.

"I represent Rick across the street," the shadow said. "How could such a beautiful girl like you reject someone like him?"

"Why do you want me?" Lucy screamed. Reaching for the light switch, she turned it on only to find the brick red refrigerator staring back at her. There was no sign of the shadow. She ran to the bathroom and switched on the light. No shadows threatened her. She rushed out of the room and opened all the closet doors. Peering in, she found nothing scary facing her.

Lucy sat down on the couch and started crying. The lights went out, and it grew cold. The heater stopped running. She curled up into a ball and huddled up against the frigid atmosphere. The shadow faced her from across the living room.

"Rick sent you that coffin as a warning. If you don't come over to his house and throw yourself at him, he'll take your soul and put it into a wax figure," the representative said. "He has the power."

Lucy shivered and wrapped her arms around her legs.

"You can't be for real!" she shouted. "Rick's home in bed."

"Call him," the shadow said.

Lucy ran for the bedroom and tripped over the bed. She grabbed the phone off its charger. Looking at it, she realized that its battery was dead. Raising her eyes, she stared face to face with the shadow. It was hovering over her face. Sharp fangs glittered as its mouth moved.

"Rick's home at his altar, waiting for you. He wants you to keep him warm."

Lucy inhaled the shadow's foul breath. She choked on the odor. Reaching behind her, she grasped the lamp. She hurled it at the shadow, who let out a shout. It staggered backward and landed with a thud. She crawled over the bed and made it for the door. Something grabbed her from behind, pulling her backward. Claws dug into her back and shoulders. Screaming at the pain, she grasped at the bedsheets.

"You won't like this," the shadow said. "I'm going to take you away."

Lucy kicked backward and hit the shadow's shins. The shadow let out a roar of pain. She whirled around and whipped the bedsheets into the shadow's face. It fell backward onto the floor.

Running for the bedroom door, she slammed it shut behind her. The shadow slid under the door's crack and followed her into the living room. She ran into the closet, closing the door behind her. Something fell onto her head. It landed with a hollow thump. Papers rustled at her feet. She picked it up and felt the letters on the book's cover.

Lucy heard the scratching at the closet door.

"You can't get away with this. Rick's magic is more powerful than yours, Lucy." the shadow sang. "He's practiced voodoo since he left New Orleans." It slid under the crack in the closet's door.

Lucy landed the thick tome onto the shadow's head. The shadow let out a gust of air.

"Now that hurt!" the shadow hollered.

She took the book and punched its head with it.

"Now wait a minute! Wait a minute!" the shadow protested. The door opened, and it fell backwards onto the floor. She fell onto it and hit it with the book. Suddenly, the lights went on again.

Lucy found herself staring down at the gold-colored carpet. The shadow disappeared.

Dropping the big, thick book, she looked down at it. It was a black leather-covered Holy Bible. Her church gave them away because they weren't relevant anymore. Someone could use it. She planned to give it away to someone for a last-minute Christmas present.

"Where are you?" Lucy shouted to the shadow. She rose to her feet and looked around her in the well-lit living room.

She went into the bedroom and sat down on the bed.

"If you come out and show yourself, I won't hurt you," she called.

"You can't hurt me. I'm made of magic. I'm coming to get you."

"You tell Rick that his voodoo doesn't work," she said.

"What are you going to do to stop me?" the shadow taunted.

"This Bible will hurt you. It's thick and heavy."

"You only can get something out of it if you believe in it!"

"Well, get ready!" she shouted to the darkness in her bedroom. "The Lord is my shepherd; I shall not want…," she read aloud.

When morning came, it found Lucy fast asleep with the Bible resting on her chest. She lay sprawled on her back, eyes shut and her glasses on the night table. A strange pile of burning material lay a foot away from her bed. The burn mark resembled the form of a seated man. The spot smelled like burning wax. The sounds of a siren screamed in the early morning air.

An ambulance roared for the house across the street. Lucy opened her eyes and got out of bed. Coming to the window, she pulled back the white curtain to see Rick being taken out in a stretcher with his head bandaged up. He wore a dazed expression as he cast his eyes up at her. She noticed that his mouth quivered when he stared at her. She didn't know if he feared her or if she imagined it.

"I'd better not tell this to my new therapist. She wouldn't believe me," Lucy muttered.

The End

Sign Off by Marc Shapiro

He saw the signpost up ahead
The sign read Don't Look Back
He did not believe in signs
He looked back
At the last thing he ever saw

Dancers in the Field by Matthew Wilson

Salem! Salem! Witches burning
Paying the price for evil learning
Death to all who spurn the light
And go witching this Halloween night.

Run
by
Hillary Lyon

A long time ago, my doctor said to me, "Kurt, with your family history of high choles-terol and heart disease, you're going to have to take up exercise, get your heart in shape. If you don't want to frequent a gym, I suggest you take up running. Your heart is a muscle. Exercise it! And watch your diet, for God's sake."

So I did. Being a wage slave, though, the only free time I had was evenings after work. I took to jogging through my suburban neighborhood, and as I built up a tolerance to pound-ing the pavement, I expanded my run into town. You'd be surprised how active our little burg is after dark, especially in the areas where the hipsters dwell.

No one paid me any mind, that is, until I ran into an old friend. Literally, as I wasn't paying attention when I rounded a corner to take a shortcut through a side street, and wham! I slammed into her and knocked us both to the ground.

It wasn't just any "her," either. It was Lisa McKay, my high school senior class prom queen. Before I could say, "Lisa McKay! What on earth are you doing back in town?" she jumped up, spry as ever, and helped me up. I busied myself brushing imaginary dirt off my clothes to hide my embarrassment.

"Why, Kurt Tollson, what a surprise!" she giggled, hiding her smile behind her well-manicured hand. It was a shy, girlish habit she'd had since elementary school. Even under the greenish streetlight, I could tell her brown eyes were as lovely as ever. Darker than I remembered, but that was probably due to the shadows cast by the streetlight.

"Tollbooth," she called me, referring to my lame teenage nickname, "you're looking ... healthy." Lisa purred, sizing me up. Okay, full disclosure: I'd been soft and a little chunky in high school. No sports for me! I was a mathlete, a brainiac with a love of pizza rolls. And Lisa. Oh, how I loved Lisa. From afar, mind you. She went steady with Kevin Selznic, our football team's all-district running back. Who was now as big as a refrigerator and had the muscle tone of a bean bag chair. How things change.

I was relieved that under the discoloring glare of the streetlight, she couldn't see me blush. "Wow! So good to see you again! You look amazing!" I laughed, more at my own clumsy, inept babble than at our serendipitous meeting. A cool master of enticing conversa-tion, I am. But it's true; she did look amazing like she had hardly aged at all.

Lisa threaded her arm through mine and suggested we go for a walk. Catch up, talk about times old and new. How could I say no? It was getting late, but what was a loss of sleep compared to hanging out with the prom queen? I grinned like a goofy teenage boy — which being around her again had turned me into — and, unable to speak, awkwardly nod-ded.

We strolled — strolled! Like characters in a romance novel — down the narrow side street towards the broader avenues that led to my home. How did she know my shortcut? I was too smitten to think to ask. Arm in arm, we waltzed down the tree-lined streets, laughing over old school gossip, sighing over current news, good and bad. We finally ran out of

"Remember when's" and "Whatever happened to's" about when we reached my front yard. I walked up to my door, fumbled for my keys. She stood behind me, so close I could smell her perfume; she was wearing something heady and vaguely incense-y. Probably a scent exotic, rare, and very expensive. That was always her style.

I opened the door and went in as she stood outside beneath the amber porch light, smiling her trademark beauteous smile. The one she wore in our senior yearbook, in the pic of her being crowned prom queen at halftime of the homecoming game. Though the yearbook's full-page spread was in black and white, her undeniable loveliness shone through and permanently burned itself into my adolescent brain. "Hey, why don't you come inside, and I'll fix you a drink. A soda, or if you like, something stronger," I said, motioning for her to enter with my outstretched hand. *Something stronger,* I berated myself, *yeah, spoken like a real smooth man-about-town.*

"I was hoping you'd ask," she replied in her sing-song voice, sweeping into my little home and lonely heart like a baleful storm cloud rolling in across the unsuspecting horizon.

****

That was years ago. How many? I've lost count; it doesn't matter, anyway. It was an era of young people's plaid shirts and shaggy hair, heroin-chic fashion models, and rising inflation. When MTV still played music videos, and presidents were held publicly accountable for their extramarital liaisons, if that tells you anything.

Lisa spent a week with me back then—it's not what you think. She was ever the perfectly chaste princess I recalled. But after high school, I learned, she'd traveled far and wide and had acquired a curious appetite one sweltering summer evening in Milan. Her experience involved meeting an older continental gentleman who, in heavily Italian-accented English, charmed her in the Piazza del Duoma. He asked her to dance to a music only audible to the two of them; a medley of violins and cellos, flowing beneath breathy altos singing lyrics in archaic Latin. Holding Lisa closely, he swirled her into the shadows of the great cathedral there, its spires sharp as glistening fangs.

One savage kiss from a stranger, and Lisa forever had a taste for, shall we say, unusual sustenance. Which she graciously shared with me during that week long ago. Lisa showed me there's a whole festering world that blooms after dark like an alluring, though malevolent, moon-flower. And this milieu existed not just in our little suburb, but in all the towns and cities beyond. It is everywhere if you know how to look.

She left me with an extraordinary new worldview—and a deeply elemental craving, one that always comes upon me during my evening jogs. Like relishing a runner's high, I'm addicted to my nightly sprees; my sluggish heart bothers me no longer, and I am in the best shape of my existence. I travel farther on foot than you would think possible and faster than you can imagine.

Recall, once upon a time, my doctor did tell me to watch my diet, didn't he? And I do, from the shadows in the evenings; I stalk as quietly as a house cat through the kitchen at midnight. I pass through their field of vision as an unsettling, amorphous fog. How do I bear their begging, their whimpers and cries, you ask me? Their whines and prayers merely spur me on, like an aural appetizer.

Moreover, I smell their fear the same way you smell meat sizzling on the grill, wafting on a summer's breeze. The arousal in the gut is the same. Every night now, as I jog, my mouth waters, my body shivers with anticipation. But most of all, most of all—and may God forgive me, because the authorities certainly won't—I love it when they run.

The End

Things the Psychic Sees by Sandy DeLuca

Shrines you've built
within black-painted walls...

Trinkets from milky blondes and
devil-eyed goth girls...
a string of pearls,
dancer's gift...
words penned by a pale-faced poet...

A Pagan priestess,
who drew a circle
around your bed...

The loves of your life...
you claimed they all went to Jersey...
when cops questioned you downtown.

But each sunrise you collect bones and dust
inside your burlap bag...
carry it through the city like a splintered cross.

And when the new moon rises
you paste bloody rags inside your book of death.

Blue Sky Somewhere
by
Marge Simon

Thea parts the curtains on the day ahead, then quickly ducks away. Sunlight unfurls from the window panes sparkling an unused coffee cup and a basket of imaginary rolls. She knows it's make-believe, a tableau laid out by habit. Useless to pretend she's one of them beyond her home, but it is all she's had for centuries.

On the floor, the shadow of a leafy oak reminds her how life struggles on outside. She'd love a glimpse of cobalt sky, a sight she treasured on the shores of Attica. Those sweet days, a memory from centuries ago when she was young, unaware her mortality was soon to change. But now, the blood of cities bleeds into a wounded sky; the atmosphere so thick with toxic fumes, few mortals dare to walk the streets without a mask.

It seems unfair that she must bear the situation, knowing it was never her intention. But worse, the shrinking population bodes her ultimate demise. She wanders darkened rooms, touching surfaces, feeling the measure of textures, the contrast of cloth and stone, glass and polished wood. Things in her small world she knows so well. Inside things, held dearly but dearer still the feel of sun on skin. A blue sky, there must be a glimpse of it somewhere.

Why wait any longer?

A twist of latch, an open door. She steps into the light.

The End

Bonfire Night by Matthew Wilson

Throw the guy upon a roaring fire
To celebrate the saving of our king
Almost killed by a vampire called Fawkes
Till our brave guards removed his wing.

The Great Swindle
by
Rod Marsden

Frank looked in the long, full-length mirror in his study. It was the one his great uncle had brought back from France at the end of the First World War. He said plaintively to it: "Who am I?"

Something fundamental was wrong. Frank's hands and face were too pale for him to be a Londoner anymore. His television screen and the movies told him so, and yet that was where he was born. If no longer a Londoner, then what was he? He couldn't imagine being anything else.

His folks had also been born in London and thought of themselves as Londoners. He remembered the singalong nights at the local drinking hole with pale ale at room temperature. Those were some good times, and no one cared back then what you looked like since Londoners could originate from anywhere.

Frank was a bricklayer, and he found work right off the bat after he left school. His granddad was in the navy and had fought back then to keep Britain free. Was Britain free now? He didn't know. He could no longer get work. That was a recent development. He was too old to join the armed services, and the local cricket team would not have him as a member anymore. He was told by one of them, "If you're brown, stick around, but if you're white, get outta sight!"

What was happening to himself and his country? He didn't know but felt the television and movie people were responsible.

The Red Lion, his favorite pub, had been closed and was not likely to reopen as a place where you could get a drink. His next-door neighbor's dog had to be put down because a new ordinance banning dogs had been introduced. The news services praised this move. There was little opposition against it.

At least his favorite Indian restaurant still served takeaway, and he could remain friends with those inside, mates that he had been at school with, and was still close to, despite what the rest of London might think of him.

He was spending too much time in front of the television screen and at the movies. What he was shown was alienating in the extreme. He was accepting of people who didn't look like him but only to a point. The line in the sand was they also had to accept him and his family's contribution to the society they were living in. He understood this contribution went back to before London was called Londinium by the Romans. They were here, his ancestors, buried throughout this large city. They had been traders, shopkeepers, soldiers, and sailors. There was change, always change. New faces, new people. That had made London great. But nowadays, he felt lost in the shuffle of this greatness.

There were forces in the media undermining what he understood to be the past, the bedrock of his very existence. Some said history had to be altered to accept others into the fold. He shook his head sadly. This was wrong. It had never happened before and should not happen now. If he was still working or his parents were still alive, he might have felt differently, not caring how much the television and the movies stuffed things up.

He remembered westerns from the 1960s in which the makers defied history, but that didn't matter because they were shows made for kids and it was Americans taking a cavalier approach to their own past and not the British. Back then, and well up to the present, British film and television crews made it their life's work to tell it like it was as much as that could be done. Now they lied! They were excluding him and the people he came from, and that did not feel good at all.

And what were the people he came from? His grandmother once spoke of a Chinese princess who had married his great grandfather and came to live in Paddington with him. She was as much a Londoner, in the end, as he thought he was up till now.

"Who am I?" asked Frank once more, a tear rolling down his cheek. The mirror didn't answer but gave an image of Elizabeth the First of England with her ginger hair, in the prime of her life, before old age and poor tooth hygiene ruined her. She was dressed so regally, in white with pearls and precious stones, the woman trying to unite Catholics and Protestants but remaining firmly a Protestant monarch. Then this queen of long ago became her movie representation. She was no longer ginger but dark everywhere. He felt his heart had been pulled out and thrown in the rubbish bin. She could no longer speak for him or to him. She wasn't the one who called his ancestors to battle. She now belonged to other people, distorting what he knew or felt he knew.

The happenstance in the mirror changed. There was Drake with his crew and ship taking on the Spanish Armada with canon at the ready. One of his ancestors might well have been there, loading canon. A magnificent moment in world history that could have gone wrong for the English but didn't. Oh, but in an instant, the Drake he knew and his crew was gone, replaced by a new, made-for television, Drake and crew. If the Spanish were defeated, who were they defeated by? Certainly not one of his ancestors anymore. "Lies and more damned lies!" he cried at the mirror. Unlike the television screen, it seemed this reflective surface was happy to give first the clean and then the severely altered history.

The mirror took him further back in time. There was King John at Runnymede about to sign the Magna Carta. The barons were all around him, urging him on. It was a swampy part of England. It was a place where it would be difficult to set a trap. The barons had on their best cloaks and so did the king. They were all Normans, nothing to do with Frank's ancestry, though a soldier present, and on guard against treachery, might have been.

A flash and the scene no longer could make sense. Yes, the Magna Carta was being signed, but by someone Frank couldn't regard as King John. The barons, too, looked odd, out of place. He was sure the Saracens hadn't conquered England. Perhaps they had in this conjured reality for television, making King John a Saracen ruler. But if he was a Saracen ruler, why did he have an English name? And what about King Richard, his brother? Didn't he fight the Saracens in the Holy Land?

The imagery in Frank's looking glass changed once more. Robin, with his band, was about to take on soldiers guarding a shipment of gold bound for London and Prince John's greedy hands. It was an ambush and the gold would either aid King Richard or help the poor. John Little, better known as Little John, was there. With him was Friar Tuck.

Little John was a Saxon yeoman, and Tuck also a Saxon. Frank understood that at least one of his ancestors had been a Saxon, and that was all right with him. Maid Marion was there in green with a bow at the ready for action and a full quiver of arrows to choose from. She was of Norman heritage but happy to fight alongside Robin in the name of King Richard. She was young and pretty with long flowing red hair. Robin was also in green with a bow, as was his men.

A distortion in the glass and more television and movie fabrications. Little John was no longer either a yeoman or a Saxon. Friar Tuck was not a Saxon or a friar but someone from Africa with strange facial tattoos. Robin and maid Marion, for now, remained the same.

Perhaps if Frank had read George Orwell's *1984*, he would have a better grasp of what was going on in the realm of show business, his mind, and the looking glass. Identity theft was happening, undermining a whole population and getting them to think and behave the way someone wants them to think and behave. It was diabolical. Gangs Frank knew of were forming, but up till now, he wanted no part of that. London should be for everyone, including himself.

All Frank understood, from his musings with that mirror, television, and the movies, was the foundations of his society were melting away under his feet like snow in Spring. He didn't like it because he, too, was melting, becoming smaller and less significant. Did he even exist in the world being recreated?

"Who are you?" asked Frank, looking at his blue eyes and pudgy nose in the mirror, his face reddening with anger. "Don't the people making the changes have their own history, their own stories to tell? Why the need to steal and then lie to everyone? Why take from me?"

If only Frank knew it wasn't the newcomers, in large numbers, doing what was being done to his sense of who he was. Most of those it was being done for were revolted by it, saying, "Indeed, we have our own past and need not borrow someone else's for any reason." They were proud of who they were and the life they were making in London.

Then Frank's head, overheated by imagery good and bad, changed his mind as to who he was and what he should do. He had to be someone and to do something about the thieves he felt had to be brought to justice.

Recently, Frank had taken up archery. He thought it would relax him. It had worked up till now. He had a compound bow and a quiver full of arrows. "I know where some of the miscreants live! That mock queen, the one who cannot be my Queen Elizabeth, resides only a few streets away." He took up the bow and quiver, saluting his mirror for its guidance, frowning at his television screen, and then leaving his humble unit.

"I am Robin of Sherwood," said Frank, proudly. If he had to be someone, let it be the famous wolf's head. He smiled for the first time in a long time. "I right wrongs. I restore history. I protect the past."

Frank knocked politely on the door of the woman who had most recently played Queen Elizabeth the First. "Who's there?" she asked.

"Special delivery," he said in a calm voice, notching an arrow.

She opened the door. She, and a dozen others within, were skewered with arrows. They flew fast. Those they were aimed at couldn't get out of the way in time. He could let fly four a minute with ease and accuracy. He had been practicing. Two of the women inside, including the fake queen, twitched before they died. He grinned in triumph over what he had done.

"At last, I know who I am!" cried Frank with glee, walking down the street, just before he was arrested by the modern version of the Sherriff of Nottingham's men. "I am Robin, and I will escape and right more wrongs!"

The End

Acheron by Sandy DeLuca

She stood on the riverbank,
bag of silver hooked on her belt,
weed and bramble at her feet.

A flock of ravens swooped above,
church bell rang deep and low,
and she shivered
when Charon waved,
his vessel piled with bones,
charms made by Bayou witches,
Voodoo hexes carved on the hull.

Dead faces
appeared in churning water--
parched lips quivered,
voices screamed for mercy.

The ferryman sang,
his voice a numinous chant,
conjuring distant stars,
and portents whispered in the dark.

Her image mirrored
in mystic water
named Acheron—
portal to the gates of Hell.

She dipped a toe into the current,
then stepped inside the roiling stream,
skeletal hands reached out--
she slid coins
on Charon's palm.

Then she was gone—
through smoke and swamp—
forever wanderer in the land of loss.

Night Gallery

Killing at the Carnival

Review by the late Tom Johnson

- Title: Killing at the Carnival "Cassie Pengear Mysteries Book #1"
- Author: L. A. Nisula
- Genre: Cozy Steampunk Mystery
- ISBN: B00RHWHOBM
- Available at: Amazon, Barnes & Noble, Kobo, and other retailers
- Price: $6.99 (eBook); 126 Pages
- Rating: 5 Stars

"A fast fun read."

Cassie Pengear, an American in London, does some typing for Scotland Yard. This usually throws her into some investigations of her own, something Inspector Burroughs wants her to stay out of. In fact, this current case she stumbles into innocently enough involves a carnival that may be mixed up in a bank robbery five years previous. Unknown to Cassie, Scotland Yard has the Kingston Carnival under observation when she takes her landlord's ten-year-old nephew to see cowboy trick shooter Nick Culpepper perform his western act. But when a person from the audience is shot dead by the cowboy in the trick-shooting act, she's in the audience to witness the killing. Ten-year-old Davy Hawkin tells her that Cowboy Nick didn't kill the victim, and it's up to Cassie to prove his innocence.

Okay, I admit it, I love stories set at the circus or a carnival, so I jumped at the chance to read this fast-moving short novel, and I wasn't disappointed. Well written, with a nice plot, and interesting characters, it kept my interest from the first page. There is no deep mystery for us to solve; it's a cozy, after all, very short and fun. A quick read in only a couple of hours, it still gives the reader their money's worth. Readers who enjoy a light mystery set in steampunk will enjoy this new series. Highly recommended.

Tom Johnson, *Detective Mystery Stories*

Payback (Mack Bolan)

Review by the late Tom Johnson

- Title: Payback (Mack Bolan)
- Author: Michael A. Black.
- Publisher: Gold Eagle Book
- Genre: Action/adventure
- ISBN: 978-0373615711
- Price: $6.99; 315 Pages
- Available at: Amazon, Thriftbooks, and other retailers
- Rating: 5 stars

Mack Bolan and Jack Grimaldi are sent to Arizona to investigate *The Wolves,* a biker organization believed to be running drugs, guns, and people across the border. There's also something going on with a weapons company named GDF that might be supplying the Mexican drug cartel with advanced weaponry. It also might tie in with a couple raids The Executioner had headed into Mexico, where the cartel was tipped off before the raid, and then another team beat the Executioner to the area. Someone in high office might be leaking their movements to someone else.

This was another topnotch adventure of Mack Bolan. This time, he may be up against super soldiers; men enhanced with a super drug to give them great strength and speed. Author Michal A. Black has walked the walk and knows the ugly business first hand. It's good to see the *Executioner* series written by someone who has been there and knows the score. Readers who like great action stories with a good plot and interesting characters will find *Payback* an exciting read. Highly recommended.

Tom Johnson, *Detective Mystery Stories*

Cop Job
Review by the late Tom Johnson

- ➢ Title: Cop Job
- ➢ Author: Chris Knopf
- ➢ Genre: Murder mystery
- ➢ Publisher: The Permanent Press
- ➢ ISBN: 978-1579623937
- ➢ Price: $29.00; 288 Pages
- ➢ Available at: Amazon, Barnes & Noble, Google Books, and other retailers
- ➢ Rating: 4 stars

"Good mystery, well written, but slow."

Alfie Aldergreen, confined to a wheelchair, is found floating in the bay with his hands strapped to the chair. He was an Army veteran suffering from PTSD and delusional. Why would anyone kill him? Sam Acquillo and Jackie Swaitkowski, two of his friends, are asked by the police chief to find out what they can about the murder. It seems that the victim was a police informer, and he wasn't the only police informer murdered recently. Then the DA calls them in. She believes there may be bad cops involved.

The case has twists and turns, with enough suspects to fill an Army platoon, and strangely, there is an Army connection hidden somewhere deep in the mystery, but what does that mean?

This well-written mystery novel kept my interest throughout, though the action was infernally slow. Oh, there was a bit of a wrestling match in the first 100 pages, then a short battle on a boat at the end of the story. It's definitely character driven, with a well worked out plot. I was able to stay with the story to the end, though at times, I wanted to toss the book in the trash. Besides being slow, the dialogue left me cold. I cannot believe men and women throw the "f" word about in everyday normal conversation and in mixed company, as if it goes on everywhere. Made me wonder if there is a quota for the "f" word now. For me, it made the characters appear unrealistic and left me wishing I hadn't read the book. Mystery lovers who can accept the unbelievable dialogue will love the mystery, however.

Tom Johnson, *Detective Mystery Stories*

Dark Pursuit

Review by the late Tom Johnson

- ➤ Title: Dark Pursuit
- ➤ Author: Jennifer Chase
- ➤ Publisher: JEC Press
- ➤ Genre: Thriller
- ➤ ISBN: 978-0991096916
- ➤ Price: $15.99 paperback; 343 Pages
- ➤ Available at Amazon, Barnes & Noble, Thriftbooks, and other retailers
- ➤ Rating: 5 stars

"Plenty of thrills to keep you on the edge of your seat."

Emily Stone and her partner, Rick Lopez, the phantom detectives, are searching for a child serial killer called *The Tick Tock Killer* by the media. He has already killed several children that are known, and maybe more that have yet to be discovered. As the story opens, Emily is in pursuit of Kevin Werner, a recent suspect in the case, when her vehicle is run off a cliff and she barely escapes. Now trailing the suspect into the woods on foot, she finds the latest victim still alive, but before she can rescue the child, Werner knocks her out and leaves her on an open grave with the bodies of other children long missing. She awakes to find the victim also dead, and wonders why the killer left her alive.

As a longtime pulp fan and researcher, I was surprised to read that the vigilante team is called *the phantom detectives.* A little later I came across this: "…what evil lurked inside him…" The 1930s through the 50s were rampant with great pulp vigilante heroes, such as The Phantom Detective, and who will ever forget The Shadow's weird announcement, "Who knows what evil lurks in the hearts of men? The Shadow knows!" I can't help but wonder if the author is familiar with the pulps. In this case, the phantom detectives, Emily Stone and Rick Lopez, are working outside the law to catch serial killers. Emily is a master profiler and ex-sheriff's deputy, while Rick was a police officer and detective, now working with Emily. There are only rumors that the phantom detectives exist. The police receive anonymous information concerning the killer once the phantom detectives have the data, then they disappear to trail another killer. It's a fascinating concept, and certainly a fun story as we follow the team of vigilantes pursuing *The Tick Tock Killer.*

Regardless of the retro connection to the pulp era, this is a contemporary setting in California, with all the computer and electronic gadgets available to the covert investigators. I did get the impression that the phantom detectives had little trust in police solving the cases. The subject matter is dark, but the writing is entertaining, and the characters move the story at a fast pace, with plenty of thrills to keep you on the edge of your seat. Highly recommended.

Tom Johnson, *Detective Mystery Stories*

Deadly Salvage (The Executioner)
Review by the late Tom Johnson

- ➢ Title: Deadly Salvage (The Executioner)
- ➢ Author: Michael A. Black
- ➢ Genre:
- ➢ Publisher: Gold Eagle Books
- ➢ ISBN: 978-0373644308
- ➢ Available at: Amazon, Thriftbooks, Blackwell of Oxford, and other retailers
- ➢ Price: $5.99; 86 Pages
- ➢ Rating: 5 Stars

"The executioner is in top form."

Mack Bolan and Jack Grimaldi are sent to the island of St. Francis to investigate the disappearance of a government code expert and his daughter. There, they discover billionaire Will Everett III supposedly filming an action movie. But corrupt police on the island harass the Americans, and Bolan discovers a team of Russian agents also on the island looking for a corrupt Russian nuclear scientist.

Plenty of action from the first page on, and The Executioner is in top form as he battles rogue Russian and American soldiers hired to start a nuclear war between the two super powers. The author knows how to write action scenes with a believable plot and characters. He creates great villains and beautiful women, with lots of bodies littering the battlefield. Fast paced, and easy reading. Highly recommended for fans of men's action series.

Tom Johnson, *Detective Mystery Stories*

Pickup at Union Station
Review by the late Tom Johnson

- ➢ Title: Pickup at Union Station
- ➢ Author: Gary Reilly
- ➢ Genre: Literary Mystery
- ➢ Publisher: Running Meter Press
- ➢ ISBN: 978-0990866619
- ➢ Available at: Amazon, Barnes & Noble, Thriftbooks, and other retailers
- ➢ Price: $16.96; 251 Pages
- ➢ Rating: 5 Stars

"A taxi ride into espionage"

A Rocky Mountain cab driver, Brandon Murphy just wants to reach his quota and go home. He doesn't drive a taxi to become rich; he leaves that to the bestseller he's going to write. Driving a cab in Denver is just to exist until the publishers discover him. Then on a rainy night, his world comes crashing down. Picking up a mysterious passenger at Union Station, he delivers him to his destination, only to discover he has a dead man in the back seat. He does everything right, and the police find out that the man simply had a heart attack, so Murph is in the clear. Then strangers come into his life, and Murph is thrown into international intrigue of spy versus counterspy, and a sinister plot is unraveled.

This was the seventh novel in the Asphalt Warrior series about Denver cab driver, Brandon Murphy. It also shows that the author could write real men's action novels, which he loved to read. This novel could easily have been written as a spy thriller from the 1960s. We have mysterious foreign spies after some deadly secret, plus the beautiful femme fatale, who might be on either side: a mysterious US Government agency, guns, and a hidden base where citizens can be secreted away for interrogation purposes and manipulation. So, fans of The Asphalt Warrior or just the writing of Gary Reilly, you will enjoy *Pickup at Union Station,* also as a taxi ride into espionage. Highly recommended.

Tom Johnson, *Detective Mystery Story*

Dyed to Death

Review by the late Tom Johnson

- ➢ Title: Dyed to Death
- ➢ Author: K.G. McAbee ~ Black Orchard Novella Award Winner
- ➢ Genre: Murder Mystery
- ➢ Publisher: *Alfred Hitchcock Mystery Magazine,* July/Aug 2015
- ➢ Cost: $7.99
- ➢ Rating: 5 Stars

The story takes place at the Grady-Best Mill Town, which is ruled by Arthur Best and his son, Jonathan Best. Hiram Alberry and his wife Esther are also workers for Arthur Best, and all become suspects in a local murder mystery. When Ida Mae Simpson is found murdered, these four have reasons to have murdered her. The victim was a loose woman and causing problems within the mill. Guy Hansen, who runs the company store, is also the mill town constable, and his young worker, Samuel C. Nicholson, assists him in the murder case. Guy was a WWI veteran, and young Sam reads pulp detectives stories and wants to become a writer of these stories.

But all their investigation proves that the four suspects were together during the time of the murder, so how could any of them be the murderer, unless …?

This was so much fun, as are all K.G. McAbee's stories. An award-winning author of many genres, I'm not surprised that she won the Black Orchard Novella Award for this mystery. I've been a fan of hers for a couple of decades now, and this novella doesn't disappoint. Highly recommended for mystery lovers of any century!

Tom Johnson, *Detective Mystery Stories*

Against the Dark Devourer

Review by Barbara Custer

- ➢ Title: Against the Dark Devourer
- ➢ Author: Margaret L. Carter
- ➢ Genre: paranormal romance
- ➢ ISBN: 979-8597187235
- ➢ Cost: $4.99 for the eBook
- ➢ Available at: Amazon. Apple, Barnes & Noble, and other retailers
- ➢ Rating: 5 Balloons

All her life, Deborah has known she and her older sister have extraordinary psi powers. When their mother dies suddenly, Deborah learns she's meant to use her gift against the forces of darkness in some unique way. How, she doesn't have a clue, but she wants no part of this alleged fate. Yet, with evil forces stalking her, can she avoid the battle ahead?

Years ago, I read Margaret L. Carter's *From the Dark Places* and loved it. I remembered hoping that she would write a sequel. This she did, titled *Against the Dark Devourer*. I opened my Kindle to read while on a bus trip and couldn't put it down until I finished. The suspense kept me flipping the screen.

Carter uses words sparingly, and when she does, she notches up the suspense. She draws the reader into the tale on page one. The story opens with the evil "Uncle Hugh" making plans to open the gates between our world and another dimension, allowing demons to enter and feed upon humans. Deborah has been gifted with strong psychic powers, and Hugh uses his protégé, Victor, to get to her. The careful way Carter draws the arc of Victor, Deborah, and Sarah impressed me. Deborah started out being rebellious against the rules of her mother and sister. But as the story progressed, she gains her agency, and little by little, by the time she confronts the dark devourer, I believe she has the strength and guts to fight. Likewise, Sara and Victor change and evolve.

This book will be understandable to readers since it centers around Victor and Deborah. However, if they want to know more about the mother and history of their psychic powers, they would enjoy reading *From the Dark Places*.

If you enjoy paranormal romances, you'll love Against the Dark Devourer. I strongly recommend this book.

Barbara Custer, Author of *The Forgotten People*

Creatures of Evil Towers by Matthew Wilson

I know she has love for me
this angel on that balcony
who sings so sweetly to only me
whose courage would secure her victory.

A nightingale locked away by cowards
sealed away so lost within this tower
surrounded by the bodies of traitors
who succumbed so easy to her power.

Her red eyes tell me all her secrets
showing me our future as one
if only I would unlock her prison cell
if I return here when the sun has gone.

Sweet Nightingale, sing your love to me
and I will then be so brave
to do what your burning eyes command
to help your voice from on your grave.

I See Red by Marc Shapiro

I don't always see well at night
But I know where the blood is
I can tell when a vein is full
And fat
And ripe for my fangs
I can spot a source a mile away
They come in all shapes and sizes
Vulnerable
Hopeful
Looking for something
Anything
In the night
At that moment I strike
Drink my fill
And continue to live
Forever
And in plain sight

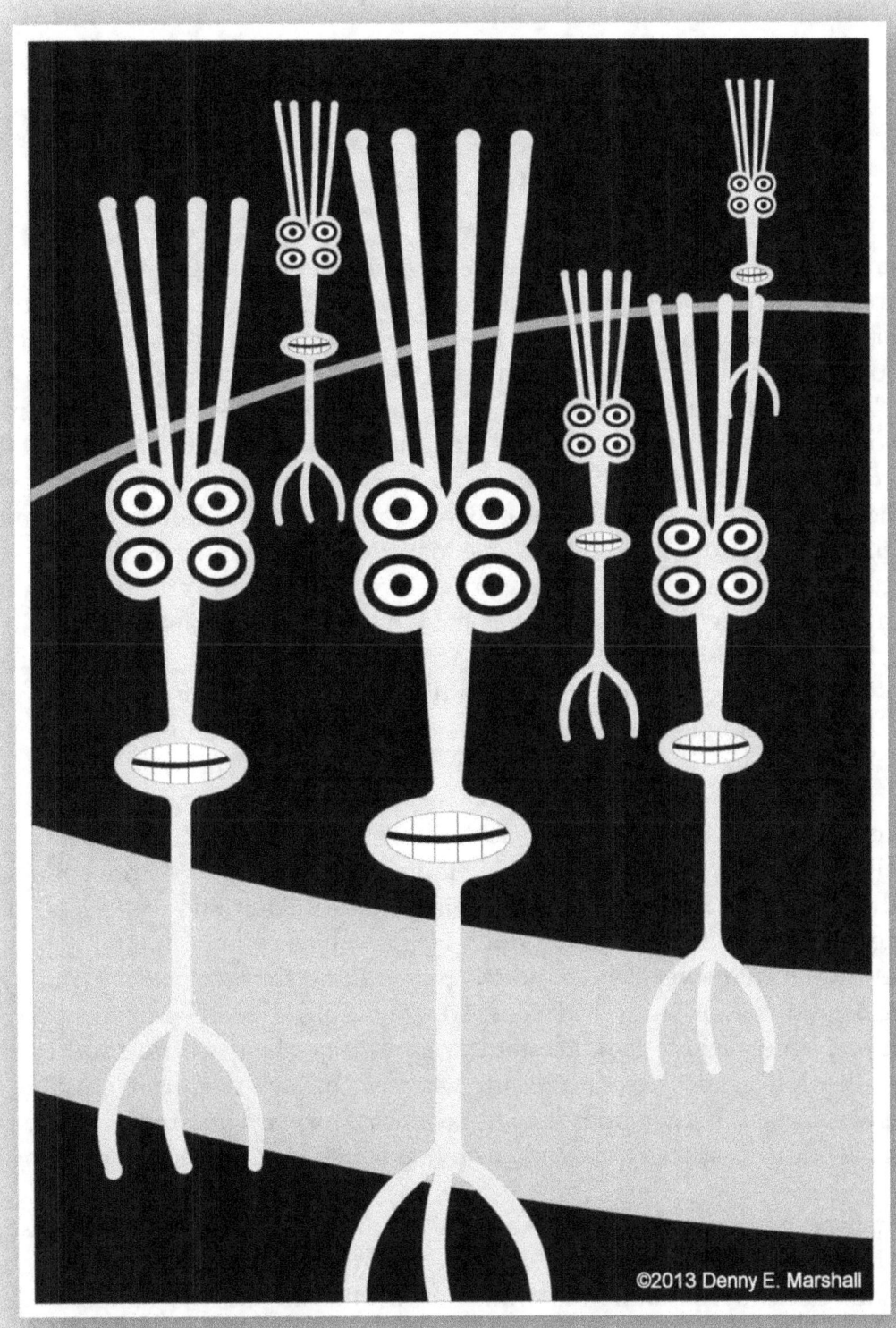

©2013 Denny E. Marshall

Mama Baoli's Doll
by
Todd Hanks

Mama Baoli is what they called her in the neighborhood. She was from the Ivory Coast of Africa, and it was well known that for a price, she would perform feats of voodoo. Her landlord Mike Wilson gave the old woman an eviction notice and informed her that she had thirty days to pack up and leave. He had no fear of her powers, not being superstitious by nature. The man also had a strong belief in Christianity. Mike thought of himself as a person who was cleaning up the block, ridding the neighborhood of bad rubbish. "I don't want the children of this neighborhood living next to witches, sorcerers, or cannibals either," he once said. He didn't know what Mama Baoli was, but he didn't like her. "I'm glad I'm finally getting rid of the old hag," he told one man as he worked in his tidy yard.

As he thrust his rake, Mike felt a sharp pain in his knee. He crumpled to the leaves. The burning sensation felt as if though someone had pushed a giant straight pin into his patella. For some reason, a vision of Mama Baoli came to his mind. "That's ridiculous," he said aloud through clenched teeth. Then a similar pain, this time in his right upper arm, knifed his being. Once again, a clear image of Mama Baoli entered his thoughts. Suddenly, Mike was not so sure he didn't believe in the power of voodoo. He had a strange feeling he was being controlled.

Mike limped down the lane and ducked behind a tall shrub just in time to watch Mama Baoli leave her small, dirty house. He thought of how he hated the antlers she had put over the doorway and her mysterious wind chimes. After she walked off down the street, Mike managed to make it to her door. He used his key and entered. Inside, bottles full of dried herbs were everywhere. Potted plants hung from the ceiling, and the inner doors were behind veils of beads. Mike gasped. On the shabby kitchen table was a voodoo doll, and it had been made to look like him. A hat like he always wore adorned the head, and around the doll's waist was his missing wristwatch. Two pins were stuck in the doll, one in the knee and one in the upper arm. Mike limped forward and removed the pins, and the pain in his body dissipated as quickly as it had come. He grabbed the doll and hurried back home.

"What should I do with the doll?" he asked aloud. "If I destroy it, won't I also destroy myself?" Mike thought long and hard. "I'll have to hide it somewhere safe," he concluded.

An idea came to his mind. Mike walked down the street to his garage. He had there a plastic cooler for camping that had a lock to keep animals from getting into the food. Mike had the only key. He put the doll in the cooler and turned the key in the lock. Now he felt safer. Mike went out to his yard to look down the street and see if Mama Baoli had returned. The house still looked deserted. Mike picked up the rake, and decided to look as if he were working, to keep an eye out for the sorceress. Suddenly his breath grew short, and he began to gasp. He fell to his knees, his face turning dusky. Like a fish tossed onto the shore, the man flopped around for a while in a pile of brown leaves, and then was still. *No air,* was his last thought. *The cooler has no air.*

The End

Symbols of the Sun by Todd Hanks

Symbol of empires and royalty,
the life force of all things.
Often in different cultures
either universal father or mother.

The Hindu god Surya
represents immortality,
and daily crosses the heavens in a
chariot drawn by horses of flame.
The vedic, Hindu demon Rahu,
captures the sun and chews,
causing an eclipse.

Khepri the ancient Egyptian
god of the rising sun
has the representation
of the scarab beetle that
rolls balls of its dung.

Rising from death flames eagle-like
the Greek myth phoenix symbolized
the end of night, of rebirth, and the
sun, its light clutching the Earth.

Haiku II by Denny E. Marshall

jack o' lantern swings
knock off frosty snowman head
replaces with its own

54

Izothaugnol Ascending
by
Lee Clark Zumpe

One

In 1947, Bernard Baruch called it a "Cold War," a clash of ideas and principles confined to rhetoric, propaganda, and aggressive diplomacy. By the time I got involved, the war was anything but cold. Skirmishes simmered in Southeast Asia, Central America, the Caribbean, and European countries just outside the Iron Curtain. Both sides employed assassination, espionage, brutal intimidation, and deliberate acts of state-sponsored terrorism to coerce developing countries into alliances.

And sometimes, the Cold War spilled over into a much older conflict.

My name is Sydney Weldon Vaughn. It would be misleading to say I was an agent for the United States. I worked for an organization ostensibly conceived of by faceless Pentagon patriots, funded by private individuals and corporations with neither national nor philosophical allegiances. Once established, the institution gradually detached itself from oversight and became a kind of elitist cabal, influencing American and Soviet politics and preventing either superpower from gaining an inequitable advantage.

In late 1961, we were just beginning to get our house in order. The world had its problems. Any day it could unthread itself, unravel into utter crawling chaos – a fate that would have amused more than a few distant spectators.

"We're at war," deputy director Eugene Bowman said, sitting on a bench on Park Avenue within walking distance of Grand Central Terminal. The lofty octagonal Pan-American building cast a long shadow. "We're not doing so well."

"The Reds are gaining momentum in this hemisphere, thanks to Castro," I said. I remember my first meeting with Bowman, thinking I had forfeited a promising military career to fight Communists in covert operations. He cleared things up that early Sunday morning.

"I'm not talking about that war, Sydney," he said, handing me a dossier. "I'm talking about something that has plagued civilization for centuries. I'm talking about external forces of unimaginable power, lingering just outside of our casual awareness, beyond our diluted senses."

"Sir?"

"Right now, all you need to know is that everything you believe is a façade, a delusion constructed to obscure the horrors of existence and the ultimate insignificance of civilization. A dark engine drives us all, Sydney, and only through vigilance and measured revolution can we hope to end the silent subjugation of the human race."

"Yes, sir." He spoke in riddles, revealing enough to win my interest without naming names or outlining strategies.

"I need you in São Paulo," he said, standing. The briefing had concluded. My first assignment I would find detailed in the documents he had provided. "Maintain your focus.

There will be distractions, things you may consider important, but you have a specific objective. You'll learn on the job. I have faith in you. You're a good soldier."

"Thank you, sir."

"Now, wait three minutes and follow me. See that drugstore on the corner?" I followed his gaze and nodded. "Give this to the man inside," Bowman said, handing me a slip of paper. "It's a prescription. That's the only place you'll want to go to get it filled. Won't cost you a cent."

Bowman walked off down the uncharacteristically empty New York City sidewalk. He was Old Guard, a veteran of the Second World War, Pacific Theater. Well into his fifties, he displayed no frailties of advancing age aside from a receding hairline and a slight limp that impeded his otherwise steady gait.

In a moment, he disappeared through the front door of the pharmacy, never looking back over his shoulder.

Three minutes later, I followed.

Inside, I found no sign of Bowman. The undersized establishment displayed no more than two aisles of medicines, including cold remedies, cough syrups, and various vitamin supplements. A young man wearing oblong glasses with thick, black frames stood behind the counter. His hair was short, boot-camp style.

"Can I help you?"

I placed the paper prescription on the wooden countertop.

"Yes, sir." He reached beneath the counter and retrieved a small, black bottle. "Have you used these eye drops before?" I shook my head, examining it. "Once a day, in the morning as soon as you get up. One drop into each eye, preferably in a dark room. Don't rub your eyes afterward, don't wash them out. You may tear up a bit. You may get a mild headache."

"What is it for, exactly?"

"It improves your vision," he said, smiling. "More accurately, it enhances it. It contains a substance that stimulates the pineal gland. The substance is cumulative. Once you've finished that bottle, the change will be permanent."

Not fully understanding his explanation, I thanked him and went on my way.

I returned to my apartment, examined the dossier Bowman had assigned to me. Transportation and lodging had been arranged. I would leave the following morning, departing from LaGuardia. Following several layovers, I would arrive in Congonhas, take a taxi into the city, check in at a little hostel in one of the city's older neighborhoods, and await further instructions.

Before leaving the next morning, I sat in my darkened studio apartment, tilted my head, and for the first time in my life, I opened my eyes.

Two

São Paulo, even in 1961, was a study in contrasting cultures. Modern skyscrapers like the Jaragua Building towered like arrogant gods over quaint old streets and buildings that dated back 400 years. The wealthiest Paulistas maintained palatial residences, their riches derived from thriving coffee empires. Meanwhile, impoverished families lived in wretched slums crawling with vermin and tainted by dark despair and resentment.

As horrible as those miserable barrios may have seemed, I saw things far worse in the days following my arrival in Brazil.

56

Had Bowman not forewarned me, I might have questioned my sanity. After the second application of the prescribed eye drops, the real world began to expose itself. I can only describe the initial feeling as one of creeping despair. Natural beauty, under a new light, revealed its inherent flaws while the uglier aspects of life became increasingly hideous.

I recognized for the first time that things are not always what they seemed to be; people are not always who they appeared to be. I saw the things that walk among us. Many remained superficially human even to my chemically expanded senses – constructed or bred to be less conspicuous, infiltrate society, and instigate chaos. Among this class, the Shadow Whisperers were most numerous. With glowing crimson eyes and sickly yellow flesh, they slipped unnoticed through crowds of people, always mumbling, always muttering, implanting seeds of fear, distrust, and hate.

They are the source of the insidious paranoia that became endemic in the second half of the 20th century.

Peeling back the grubby curtain and peering out the window, I saw them weaving through the crowded marketplace in the streets below, things that should have existed only in the shadows of nightmares walking transparently amongst townsfolk in the middle of the day.

"You're Vaughn, right?" My Brazilian contact found me cowering in my cramped dwelling a few days after I arrived in the city, still wrestling with the effects of the drug. "Taking your eye drops like a good *guerrero, si*?"

"Yeah."

"*Bueno, señor.*" He sat at the foot of the bed, threw me a handkerchief to mop the sweat on my face. "You'll get used to it. Doesn't take long. My name is Gaspar, by the way," he said, introducing himself. "You're in good hands here. The caretakers are sympathetic to the cause. They understand."

"Agents?"

"No, just plain folk," he shook his head. "Not everyone needs the eye drops to see what's out there. Some people have naturally heightened senses. Call it intuition, clairvoyance, extrasensory perception, or sixth sense."

"How can they handle it?"

"Most don't. Most end up in asylums." Even though my exposure up to that point had been limited, I remember thinking that insanity might be less troublesome than acceptance. "Poor bastards, no one believes them – but they're right, and the rest of the world is blind."

"Where do they come from?"

"Oh, they've been here all along. We've just gotten better at recognizing them." From his build and manner, I could tell he was only a few years my senior, but he wore his worries on his face. Whatever hardships and heartbreaks he had suffered had aged him prematurely. Gaunt and gangly, his skin was darkly tanned like a rolled cigar. His eyes retreated into dark, burnished pits. Once, he may have been handsome. Seeing those things had eroded his features, worn away at his veneer. "Generally, coexistence is viable – even beneficial in some ways. Occasionally, something steps over the line, usually by invitation. A situation arises, and we must step in and put things right."

"Balance the scales?"

"Precisely."

"And that's why I've been sent here," I said, dismissing a wave of nausea. "I'm supposed to assassinate one of those things."

"Well, you can try, but I wouldn't put my *cruzeiros* on you." He chuckled, but the smile evaporated quickly. "By our standards, these things are practically immortal and virtually invincible. Slow 'em down a little, sure. Kill 'em – good look, it's your funeral."

"Then what – why was I brought here?"

Gaspar stood, searched his pockets. He took out and unfolded a grainy black and white surveillance photo of a burly middle-aged man wearing an unbuttoned, long sleeve shirt. The picture had been taken from a distance and showed the man addressing a group of native Brazilians in an outdoor setting, possibly a village in the jungle. I recognized him immediately.

"You're familiar with Maximilian Vogel, *si*? He goes by the name Mueller now, Luca Mueller."

"Yes." My assignment began to make sense. I had helped the American military ferret out former Nazis in the last few years, taken part in cooperative manhunts with the British and Israelis. Some subjects were terminated, some brought to trial. One I smuggled back to the United States after faking his death – I had been ordered to return him so that he could be persuaded to serve the American government. "He's here? In São Paulo?"

"In Santos, actually, about forty miles from here," he said, gazing out the window. His initial friendliness began to dissipate, replaced by growing unease and anxiety. He scanned the streets below, searching for something. "We must complete our business *rápidamente, señor*."

"What does he have to do with all this?" Vogel, a notorious war criminal and former Nazi, had committed acts of singular degeneracy and depravity so appalling that even some of his contemporaries branded him a butcher. Fürchtegott and Verschuer labeled his experiments grotesque and "of dubious scientific value" but never lifted a finger to halt them. Only Matthias Batsdorff, another infamous Nazi butcher parading as a scientist, supported his so-called research - terrifying and pointless tests performed on gypsies that amounted to nothing more than torture. "Has he formed some kind of alliance with those things?"

"Worse," Gaspar said. "He's managed to stir a powerful being, provoked him into ending centuries of dormancy and rekindled his inclination for worship and sacrifice. Tonight," he continued, "he'll attempt a ceremony that will allow Izothaugnol to exploit weaknesses in barriers that have kept him from physically returning to earth."

"He can control this thing?"

"Of course not, but he thinks he can. They always think they can control them."

Gaspar cautiously retraced his steps, backing toward the door. Sensing my confusion, he gestured toward the window, and I warily surveyed the scene. "We've got company."

Wearing tan uniforms, three men marched through the crowd, defiantly eyeing the natives with embedded loathing. Blond-haired, blue-eyed constructs of fabled eugenics experiments, these men had come for me – to make sure I never came close to finding Vogel. As if to provide evidence of their collaboration with those "exterior forces" Bowman had mentioned, a hoard of hovering monstrosities followed their lead.

Gaspar motioned toward the door as he pulled out a Ballester Molina M1916, an Argentine clone of a Colt M1911 .45 caliber.

"What are those things?" Looking like winged, black caterpillars, each creature had a four long, spindly spider-like legs protruding from the spot where its eyes should have been. Beneath the grasping appendages was a puckered, ovular mouth lined with thorny teeth.

"A Seething Swarm," Gaspar said, flinching. "You've heard of our piranha? Same principle, only less friendly and airborne."

Instants later, machinegun fire echoed through the old hostel, generating a torrent of screams from frightened townsfolk in the street. Without hesitation, I grabbed my gear and prepared to follow Gaspar.

"Got a weapon?"

"I thought you said you can't kill them."

"*Sí*," he said, smiling. "But you can kill zealots."

Three

In our exodus from São Paulo, we left a grisly mess at the hostel – one the local authorities would be forced to unravel or conceal. Gaspar may have been well-informed and instinctive, but he possessed wretchedly poor shooting skills. Vogel's men had already infiltrated the establishment's first floor, and we found them in the long hallway leading from the front to the back door.

Gaspar scattered several indiscriminate shots down the corridor, most of them ending up embedded in the walls and ceiling.

"Sorry, *señor*. I'm much better with a machete."

Brandishing German MP 35 submachine guns – a favorite of Hitler's elite Waffen SS during the war – Vogel's assassins began a systematic sweep of the first floor. Having alerted the death squad to our presence, we had no choice but to finish the job quickly and efficiently. Though no words were exchanged between us, it became evident that Gaspar expected me to handle things.

After finding adequate cover for my gun-shy acquaintance, I drew my Walther P38K and put all three down with little effort.

The Seething Swarm dispersed upon their demise, deprived of direction. Sadly, the hostel keepers had already fallen victim to them. We found their remains in a pile of bloody bones in the office. Another ten guests had been gunned down in the melee, and the sirens of approaching *policia* bemoaned the carnage.

We managed to slip out into the streets of São Paulo unnoticed.

On the two-hour drive to Santos, speeding down some 2,500 feet on winding roads, along hairpin turns, and across chasm-spanning bridges, Gaspar initiated me into this new world. According to him, Izothaugnol was a Great Old One, a member of an extraterrestrial, hyper-dimensional race that colonized Earth long before the rise of sentient life. He explained as much of the history as he thought I could manage given my naïveté in the field.

"Most recently, Izothaugnol had worshippers in the Xingu region, indigenous peoples that performed elaborate ceremonies well into this century. The Juruna recognize it as an elemental force but do not deify it like other tribes." He said that Izothaugnol had been depicted in stone carvings as seven intertwined serpents with a single head, twenty-one eyes, and a mouth ringed by tentacles bristling with needle-like quills. Regional folklore suggests that he can reverse the flow of the seasons, and at least one European grimoire attributes to him the power to transport acolytes through time portals. "His cult center was based in Goiania until Vogel moved it to Santos."

"But if Izothaugnol cannot physically appear, how did the natives learn to worship it?"

"Good question. It communicates with select individuals through dreams. The natives consider sleep a kind of temporary death, and dreams are another world, separate from this. In that world, Izothaugnol can connect with them."

"What about Vogel? How did he end up here?"

"Why do you think so many Nazis fled to South America? Look around you." In the dense forest lining the steep terrain on either side of the roadway, I saw ancient shrines not visible to the untrained eye. Upon an adjacent hilltop, I recognized a step pyramid all but reclaimed by nature, its crowning altar long abandoned and thirsty for blood. "They came not only to escape prosecution." Many war criminals – particularly the so-called academicians – were known to have dabbled in the occult, mixing science and magic and exploring arcane lore and eldritch teachings. "They came here to continue their work, to put themselves in a position to communicate with dark forces."

Skeletons of ancient, wicked cities dotted the jungles, indistinguishable to the ordinary people but excruciatingly evident to one with enhanced powers of perception. Shielded from detection by sophisticated alien technology or residual psychic energies, Gaspar explained that the ruins harbor unspeakable horrors, things that may well reemerge over the coming decades as the reckless pursuit of natural resources pushes plunderers deeper into the wilderness and the borders of rainforest continue to contract.

"Vogel and the others exploited the mythology of the indigenous peoples to establish a new religion." A decade and a half of manhunts had led to developing countries where pagan worship flourished in remote areas. My own experience tracking war criminals left me without a doubt. I began to connect the dots. Certain members of the Nazi elite had specialized in plundering Europe's libraries, museums, and private collections, appropriating relics and gathering esoteric literature. "These men always had a hidden agenda. They didn't care which side won the war. They just wanted to divert attention from their own actions."

"Now you're catching on," Gaspar nodded.

I realized my previous ignorance kept me blissfully oblivious. History became a tangled sequence of lies and half-truths, religions a prop, philosophy a distraction. Like darkness visible, the shadows plaguing our progress, prodding us into unwanted wars and rampant nationalism and ethnocentrism became as clear as the veiled entities stalking us.

"If they challenge us, how can we mount a defense?" I turned to Gaspar, who returned my blank stare. "If they already control us, how can we hope to stage a successful rebellion?"

"Destiny, some say, is written in the stars," Gaspar said. He pointed toward the eastern horizon, the band of purple hovering above the Atlantic heralding nightfall. "Their powers ebb and flow like the cyclic tides. Until the stars are right, they cannot recapture their former dominion. They can only influence civilization, obstruct us from achieving our potential before they reunite."

The early signs of dusk had begun permeating the skies as we approached the seaport of Santos. As the distant stars emerged like celestial candles illuminated by unseen hands in the cathedral of twilight, I gazed skyward, momentarily transfixed by the vastness of the cosmos. Tiny points of sparkling light crowded the night sky, falsely portraying a universe teeming with life. In reality and by our technological standards, the great abyss of vacuous space and dark matter made each galaxy an inaccessible atoll, each star an isolated island. In that immeasurable void, the earth was but a speck of dust.

Driving down centuries-old streets through a city settled less than a hundred years after Columbus sailed, we proceeded in uncanny silence. Gaspar had revealed as much as he could. I had resigned myself to the hopeless crusade.

We approached the darkened harbor, parked alongside an immense warehouse. By day, tobacco, bananas, processed sugar, rubber, and coffee flowed through this busy port, traveling to America, Europe, Asia, and Africa.

Dockside, we found a group of men – brothers of those we had left for dead in São Paulo – standing guard outside a derelict tanker. The shadows concealed other less tangible sentries, things my eyes strained to detect. I followed Gaspar as he found adequate cover behind a mountain of crates. On deck, a single silhouette leaned against the ship's railing.

"That's Vogel," I whispered, but Gaspar lifted a hand to silence me.

I heard the squeal of tires on the pavement before I saw the headlights. A car sped into the shipyard, screeching to a standstill on the other side of the crates only yards from where we had hidden.

Vogel shuffled down the gangplank, approached the vehicle tentatively. One man stepped out of the car, facing the war criminal. With his back to us, I could not identify him. Following abridged salutations, a brief conversation ensued. The car's engine muffled their voices, burying the substance of their heated dialogue. However, Vogel's spirited gestures and dissatisfied scowl attested to a bitter and escalating disagreement between the two men.

"This is unexpected," Gaspar said softly. "And unfortunate."

"Do you know who the other man is?"

"I have an idea."

Vogel snapped his finger, and all his guards scrambled, lining up in formation behind him. Vogel stepped to one side. A torrent of machinegun fire cut the seven fanatical servants down where they stood.

"I can kill them both from here,"

"Not yet – the ceremony has already begun," Gaspar said, frowning. His face seemed clouded with disappointment; his eyes flooded with unshed tears. "We go through life thinking we shape destiny when we only play roles we were born to play."

The man from the car looked over his shoulder, scanned the darkness where we crouched. My fingers teased the cold steel of my sidearm. His face remained concealed, cloaked by a black veil. Turning back to Vogel, he produced a shining cylindrical object from his pocket – a translucent, pulsing shaft that resembled polished quartz but possessed an almost alien aspect.

Vogel held out his hands, his palms upturned. He gazed upon the object with a mix of ecstatic reverence and maniacal anticipation. I think he may have giggled, overcome with rapturous bliss and exhilaration.

Behind them, the bodies of the men began to transform. As shadow retreated from the growing luminosity of the object, their forms elongated and softened, their features melted into memory. Their limbs merged and their bodies distended and undulated unnaturally, and their flesh reformed as snakeskin.

A sphere of light now expanded from Vogel's cupped hands, radiating outward, swallowing the car, the crates, and the ship's bow. At its center, I saw a serpent's head; I saw Izothaugnol forming, fusing with seven writhing bodies squirming in the shipyard.

The man wearing the veil backed away from Vogel, away from the dock.

"You see the object Vogel is holding? In a minute, he'll disappear – at that moment, I need you to shoot that thing – shatter it into a million pieces. I will handle Vogel – it is more important that you destroy the object." Gaspar wept openly now. At the time, I thought he feared the ceremony had gone too far – that he could not stop Izothaugnol from returning. Machete in hand, he leaned forward, readying himself for an action I could not have anticipated. "You are a good *guerrero, señor.*" He tucked a slip of paper in my shirt pocket, patted me on the shoulder. "Prove me wrong. Find a way to change destiny."

Gaspar charged into the pulsing light, tackling Vogel. The men instantly vanished.

"Gaspar!" I screamed, abandoning my cover. The crimson eyes of Izothaugnol glared at me, its seven tails thrashing with vibrant life. Ignoring its hypnotic gaze, I took aim and fired. A single shot ran out, and the shining cylindrical object burst into a shower of glittering shards, like millions of shimmering stars almost frozen in time, descending and slowly fading.

Izothaugnol evaporated instantly, unable to complete his materialization, banished again from this world and forced into exile to await the next invitation. Its premature departure preempted the hideous metamorphosis that would have provided its seven serpentine bodies, leaving behind the dying forms of seven men combined into one shuddering and bleeding mass. With seven mouths, it screamed, and its shriek will echo through my mind until death mercifully dismisses it.

Four

Days later, I found myself in a little library in the town of Santos. The events that had transpired had been reported as multiple homicides. Speculation leaned toward smugglers. Investigators had no leads.

The black-veiled man had disappeared. I never discovered his identity.

The slip of paper Gaspar had deposited in my pocket stated the name of the library and included a file number. I approached the reference desk casually, placed the piece of paper on the countertop.

"*Por favor?*" The woman behind the counter smiled and nodded.

A few minutes later, she returned with a copy of a local newspaper. Not knowing what to look for, I thanked her and retired to a table in an empty corner of the building where I could examine the periodical uninterrupted.

Dated late September, 1939, I scanned the headlines. Much of the front section detailed recent events in Europe, devoted to coverage of Germany's invasion of Poland and annexation of Danzig. World War II had begun.

I found what I was looking for buried in the second section. An unnamed man had been shot to death by local police after he was found crouching over the mutilated body of a foreigner near the docks. An artist's sketch of the victim and suspect accompanied the story.

In return for summoning Izothaugnol, Vogel had arranged to go back in time, perhaps thinking he could alter the outcome of the war. Izothaugnol had obliged his whim. Armed with foreknowledge, Gaspar kept Vogel from achieving his objective.

Gaspar had circled his picture. He left a message for me, too.

"Vogel won't get a second chance. History can't be rewritten. It's up to you to find out if the future is equally inflexible."

Unconvinced that my continued service would have any impact on the fate of civilization, I still carried out my duties for the next several decades, serving humanity's best interests to the best of my knowledge. I strived to live up to Gaspar's challenge, hoping to find evidence that we are not simply executing predetermined actions like puppets with unseen masters.

As I near the end of my limited immortality, having faced the unmasked horrors of this world, I still cannot resolve one mystery. I would like to believe my life was my own.

Staring into the cathedral of twilight, watching as the celestial candles slowly burn away toward the great blackness at the end of time, I pray that I am not a mere cog in an invisible machine driven by some dark engine I cannot hope to comprehend.

The End

Ales Stenar by Lee Clark Zumpe

faceless ancestors toil in
bronze age fields across Europe
erecting megalithic monuments

imprinting cryptic messages
that echo across millennia
and beguile distant descendants.

near Kaseberga they still stand
provoking dubious speculation
about gods in fiery chariots

providing technological innovations
in return for veneration
and the promise of immortality.

Primal Vampire
by
Marge Simon

I loved him once, my fair-haired giant of a guy. His name was Martin before he was turned. He insists we call him Alexander, now.

Tall to start with, he's grown two inches since the Change. He's discovered the Primal Scream, only now it's the Scream of the Undead, or so he claims. We are compelled to gather when he calls.

It's insane, it's not our normal way at all. I remember that book by Mr. Matheson, *I Am Legend*. Actually, Alexander must remember it too, since we read it together in college. In it, the vampires came at night, plaguing mortals hiding in their houses. That's what Alexander expects of us. It isn't right, staking out houses, wailing at the doors and windows to frighten them. Of course, we're impervious to bullets, we have no fear of them, nor fire or bombs. Alexander has become so powerful, we must comply. When the mortals finally step outside, we're at their throats.

Yes, I loved him once. But he was my sweet Martin then. I don't know him anymore. This evening, I watch as he throws back his head, roaring a summons. Dark clouds are gathering, and the wind is suddenly bitter cold.

The End

Noorie
by
Jon M. Fox

Sam Edwards had not seen what had happened, but he heard about it the next day. Everyone was talking about it. It seems that a woman from Begunkodar, the village where he was living, had died horribly. Sam had occasionally seen the woman waiting to board the train to Purulia every couple of weeks or so when he collected some packages sent from overseas by his parents. Sam heard the woman was crossing the tracks to get a ticket at the Begunkodar station at about 3:15 p.m. that day. As she crossed the double set of tracks, somehow, her white saree got caught in one of the fasteners holding the rails to the sleepers. She struggled to free herself, but she couldn't pull her saree loose.

The afternoon express from Ranchi doesn't stop at the Begunkodar station on its way to Howrah Junction. The woman first heard the wires overhead humming. She looked up and saw the train coming down the track. She started screaming for help. The stationmaster, who had come on duty just a short time earlier, looked out of the window of his office and saw the woman pulling on her saree. But he dismissed it from his thoughts as he worked on totaling the receipts from the previous day. Nearby, there were some field hands working in one of the rice paddies who heard her cries. They looked up and saw the woman on the track and ran towards her through the water-filled paddy. The train sounded its horn as it sped towards the station. Onboard the train, the engineer saw the woman struggling and again blew the horn as he applied the brakes. But it was already too late. The woman made one more terrible scream. The stationmaster looked up from his desk out the window. He saw the train hit her.

There was not much left of the woman by the time the train had managed to stop. Everyone near the station was horrified at what had happened. A few people at the station looked at the blood smeared on the rails and at the pieces of bloody white cloth and flesh scattered down the track. The men from the rice paddy were crying as they tried to console themselves over their failure to help. Some of the people who were there later related all of this to Sam. They also told him that the stationmaster couldn't help himself as he fell to the ground and vomited the remains of his earlier meal out of his stomach.

The name of the woman in the white saree was Noorie, meaning "light" in Hindi. She was said to be a close relative of Lachan Kumari, a queen of a group of the local Santal Tribe. This queen was the same woman who had donated the land for the station around 1960. Why Noorie was dressed in white was unknown, as the Santals traditionally dress in multicolor clothing, with a turquoise blue or red and green saree being a favorite. But she was said to always wear white when seen in public. Some thought that perhaps it was somehow related to her given name, and the fact that she was of much fairer skin color than most other Santal.

Noorie's relatives came to the station to claim what was left of her. Her remains were cremated, and the pieces of bone were placed under the rafters of her family house, according to Santal custom. There they would remain, to be taken out for certain rituals during the next three years, while her spirit, or *bonga* in the Santali language, roamed between worlds.

Sam had been in Begunkodar for just over a year in his two-year posting with the Peace Corps. He had come there in early 1966 and was enjoying the cultural experience. Just a few years ago, he would never have imagined living in the Purulia District of West Bengal, India. Life in Begunkodar was so different from his upbringing in California, but he did not regret the choice he made in his senior year at Humboldt State University to sign up as a volunteer following his graduation. His specialty was in appropriate technology engineering, and he was supposed to bring new ideas and methods to improve the old traditional methods of growing rice and other crops and help in different ways to improve the lives of the villagers. So far, he had little success in getting the people to try out new things, but he was now fairly well accepted in the local community as a welcome resident.

A few days after the accident, Sam went to the train station to see if a package he was expecting had arrived. It was late afternoon, and the stationmaster was preparing for his nightly shift in the ticket room. Even in the evening, it could be busy at the station. Quite a few trains either stopped or went by in the evening and early morning hours. From talking with him on earlier visits, Sam found that the stationmaster enjoyed his position immensely, but something about him seemed different this evening. Sam was still learning Santali, but his Hindi was pretty good now, and the stationmaster spoke Hindi and fairly good English.

"Good afternoon, sir," said the stationmaster in formal English as Sam came to the ticket window.

"Good afternoon to you as well, Mohan," said Sam in his best Hindi.

"Ah, Sam *sahib*, I have a package here awaiting for you," Mohan continued in English.

"Thank you very much, Mohan," said Sam. "I was expecting it to arrive today. That is why I am here."

"Yes, yes - the package came earlier today. My assistant brought it here to keep safe for you. I always keep it here in the office for you," said Mohan.

As the stationmaster picked up the package and opened the door for Sam to get it, Sam looked at Mohan and noted he seemed rather nervous or anxious about something. As soon as Sam picked the package up, Mohan closed the door to the ticket office and quickly locked it.

"Mohan, what seems to be bothering you this evening?"

"Nothing yet this evening, *sahib*, but it was last night I saw something. Something I cannot believe. But still, I believe... It was her, *sahib*. I know it was her. You know, the woman in the white saree. It was Noorie I saw."

Mohan began to shake as he continued speaking to Sam.

"It was a later than now. The local train from Ranchi had just come. A few people got off. The train began to move again. Then I saw her. Wearing the white saree. She was running along the side of the train like she wanted to get aboard. Then she vanish. She was there and then she gone in that instant."

"Are you certain of what you saw?" asked Sam.

"I know what I see. It is the woman. The same in the white saree. So now I lock the door so she will not touch me."

"A good measure of protection," said Sam, as he tried to figure out what the stationmaster might have actually seen. Of course, it couldn't have been Noorie.

As Sam got ready to leave, he said, "You take care, Mohan. I am expecting another parcel to arrive soon, so I will see you in a few more days to see if it is here."

As Sam walked out of the doorway of the station, Mohan said, "See you later, *sahib*."

Sam walked back to his motorbike, started it, and drove toward the village, carrying his package on the back rack. He hoped that this was the one that had coffee in it, as he had run out a few weeks earlier. *If not this package, it will be in the other one,* he thought to himself.

After riding his motorbike about four and a half kilometers on Duarsini Road, Sam reached the edge of the village, drove past the Hari Mandir Temple, and turned down the short street to the house where he was staying. He shared the house with a local family who were paid a stipend for his lodging and meals. It was a comfortable arrangement.

Retiring to his room, Sam started thinking about the stationmaster's words about what he had seen. Surely, it must have been someone else that he saw. Noorie was no more, that was certain. As Sam prepared for bed, he forgot about the incident as he thought of the smell of hot brewed coffee in the morning. He had found the coffee in the package he had picked up, and he knew it was going to be a better day tomorrow because of it.

The next afternoon, Jitendhar Kisku, one of Sam's housemates, found Sam working with a villager on devising a better way to move water from an irrigation channel to a rice paddy. Jitendhar was about the same age as Sam and spoke excellent English, having attended school in New Delhi. As he saw Sam, he yelled towards him, "Sam! Sam! Have you heard about the train station?"

Catching up with Sam, Jitendhar said, "Sam, my friend. Have you heard about the stationmaster? He is telling everyone that last night he saw the woman that was killed by the train last week. He said she was dancing inside the station and laughing at him. He was quite serious, you know. But he also is said to be very frightened. At least that is the story being told."

"Jitendhar, who did you hear this from?" asked Sam.

"I have heard it from several people in our village. It seems that some of those passengers that arrived at the station early this morning found the stationmaster locked in his office and refusing to answer when he was called. He eventually came out and told them what he had seen the previous evening."

"Yes, he told me last afternoon when I picked up my package. He said the previous evening he had seen the woman running alongside the train like she was trying to get on board. He said that she then just vanished."

"It must be the woman's *bonga*. It must be her spirit that is roaming near the station!" exclaimed Jitendhar, sure of his assessment. Sam knew from what he had learned while at Begunkor that a *bonga* were spirits that lived between the world we can see, *Noa Puri*, and *Hana Puri*, the world that we cannot see but is still connected to the visible world.

Sam listened to Jitendhar and formed his own opinions of the situation. As he and Jitendhar were talking, the *goret*, the messenger of the village headman, walked by and heard them discussing the situation at the train station. He stopped for a moment, and at a break in the conversation, cleared his throat, indicating he had something to say. He spoke too rapidly in Santali for Sam to catch all the words, but when he finished, both Sam and Jitendhar bade him farewell. As the *goret* continued walking toward the village proper, Sam asked Jitendhar what the *goret* had said.

"He says that Mohan has put in for a transfer. So, to try and keep him from leaving, the village *manjhi*, or headman, has asked the *goret* to obtain the assistance of an *ojha* in trying to appease the *bonga* of the departed woman," Jitendhar explained.

Sam knew that an *ojha* performs magical rites and is supposed to know a *bonga's* wishes. He would do some chanting of *jharni mantar* to try to get the *bonga* to stop its trouble-making.

The villager that Sam was working with took all this conversation in, with eyes wide and mouth open, and then said to Jitendhar in Santali that he hoped that the work of the *ojha* would be successful. Jitendhar agreed and started walking back towards the village while Sam and the villager resumed their work.

Two days later, and four days after the death of Noorie, it was time for Sam to check on the second package he was expecting. Besides some American razor blades and a couple of cans of peaches, Sam was looking forward to receiving a box of dehydrated mashed potatoes. He was getting tired of just having rice all the time and also wanted to share a little American food with his housemates. Sam took off on his motorbike in the late afternoon, making the journey on Duarsini Road on his way to the train station.

When Sam arrived, he found Mohan in the ticket office with the door locked. Mohan didn't look good. He looked like he hadn't been getting enough sleep, and there were dark circles around his eyes.

"Mohan," said Sam. "You look like you have been here at the station ever since I last saw you."

"No *sahib*. I have gone home every morning when my assistant comes into the station to take over my duties."

Mohan continued with his story, saying, "Every night I see the woman. She dances and sings in the station lobby. Then she points her hand towards me and beckons me to join her. No one else is here to see her. Only me. I lock myself in my office so she can't touch me. I know it is the spirit of Noorie. It is her ghost, I think that you say in English."

"*Mujhe bhooton par vishvaas nahin hai,*" cried Sam in Hindi, that he didn't believe in ghosts, trying to change Mohan's viewpoint. But Mohan was convinced that he had been seeing the woman's spirit and would not be convinced otherwise. He told Sam that he was going to transfer to another station in three more days and be replaced by a new station manager.

"But Mohan, I am sure that this situation will get better. I hear that the village is sending an *ojha* to reason with the woman's spirit and convince her *bonga* to leave," Sam explained.

"No, my friend," said Mohan. "I will be leaving soon. It is too much for me to bear, seeing this woman's spirit wanting me to come with her. I must go soon. It is better."

"Are you sure, Mohan? I will certainly miss you, my friend. Perhaps you can send me a letter from your new station. I have enjoyed our conversations, and your English is even getting better because of it."

"Thank you, *sahib*," said Mohan. "I will certainly send you a message when I secure my new position." Mohan looked behind him in the ticket office and picked up a parcel. "Ah! Here is the package you are expecting, my friend," said Mohan, smiling once again as he opened the door and handed the package to Sam.

Sam tied the package to his motorbike and rode back to the village. He was sorry that his friend at the station was leaving, but there was nothing he could say to help with the situation. Mohan was convinced that he had to go.

Three days later, before the sun had even risen, Sam was awakened by a lot of men's voices speaking loudly, and some women crying, some even screaming. He got up, put on his khaki shorts and a shirt, slipped his sandals on his feet, and went outside. Jitendhar was outside their house. Sam walked up to him and asked what was going on.

"Sam, my friend. I am sorry to say that Mohan has died," Jitendhar said bluntly.

"How did it happen?" asked Sam.

"They are saying that last night, sometime after 10:00 p.m., the *ojha* arrived at the station to chant the *jharni mantar* to reason with the woman's *bonga*, but when he arrived, he could not find anyone there at first. Then he looked in the stationmaster's office. The door was open, and he could see Mohan there, on the floor of the office. He eyes were open, and he had a look on his face that showed he had seen something terrible. But he was dead, Sam. His body was still warm, so he had died not too long before the *ojha* arrived. The *ojha* left the station and quickly walked back to the village, and told the headman what he had seen at the station. Of course, in short order, many in the village knew of what had happened. So now, almost everyone knows," Jitendhar explained. "They are even saying that the *bonga* of Noorie is a *Bhujni Budhi*, or a female demon," said Jitendhar. "It is being said that Noorie's *umul*, her shadow, fell upon Mohan and brought the accident - the *daram* - that resulted in his death."

"What a terrible thing to happen to Mohan," said Sam. "Has someone examined his body to determine exactly how he died?" Sam didn't believe in ghosts or spirits, so he knew there was some other reason behind Mohan's death.

"No, Sam. Everyone is afraid to go near him," said Jitendhar. "So, a medical officer from the government has been summoned. He will surely find out how he died. But I think it was that spirit of that woman who did it at the station. She must have touched him and drawn away his life."

"Yes, Jitendhar, I am sure that is what people here will believe," said Sam. "But I think that he must have had a stroke or heart attack. Perhaps from the stress of his fear of this woman's spirit, whether it exists or not."

"Of course, Sam. I know that you have your beliefs about these things, but we have our beliefs also," said Jitendhar.

The people in Begunkodar talked about the circumstances of Mohan's death for the rest of the day, and as evening approached, the streets cleared, as people went to their homes before it got dark. Sam also was home before dark that evening. After he and Jitendhar finished their evening meal with Jitendhar's family, they went to Sam's room to talk a bit and drink some homemade *handi*, the local rice beer.

"Sam," began Jitendhar, "there are some of the people here that believe that the woman Noorie was a *dain*. I think the English word you use for that kind of person is a witch. She always dressed in a white saree, and she herself was pale in skin, much like you - but of course, that does not mean that you are a *dain*."

They both laughed at that as the *handi* began to relax them.

"Why would the way she dressed or looked make people think she was a witch?" asked Sam.

"It is not just how she appeared that people consider," said Jitendhar. "It is because she is a woman, and related to the queen of a group of our people. How do you think Lachan Kumari got her power and place among our people? It must be through her powers as a *dain*. Have you not heard the story of how Santal men requested that *Maran Buru*, one of our greater spirits, teach them the ways of a *dain* so they could use it to control their women? It is said that the women heard of this request and dressed up as their husbands. While the men were all sleeping, the disguised women met with *Maran Buru* and he taught them the ways and powers of a *dain*. Later, after *Maran Buru* discovered he had taught the women how to be a *dain* instead of the men, he taught the men how to become *ojhas*, and how to discover if a woman is a *dain* and make the right sacrifices and appeasements to counter a *dain* and her powers."

"I hadn't heard that story before," said Sam.

"Yes, Sam. That is the way of our people and their beliefs. Even those that have gone to university believe this. That is why you don't see women entering the *Jaher Garh*, our area where we offer sacrifices and tribute to the spirits. They are usually forbidden, as they might gain more power from the *bonga* if they are a *dain*."

"No one explained that to me before," said Sam.

Sam thought about this, and it explained a lot. He had noticed women did not take a regular place in the ceremonies he had seen, but had just thought it was part of the culture and how men maintained their power and control in the village. Now he knew that it was a means to keep women from becoming more powerful than they already were. That also explained how a queen could be far more powerful than the village *manjhi*, even though the headman kept the village organized. Seemingly, it was the women that had the most power in the village. They only appeared subservient to the men.

As Sam and Jitendhar continued to talk, Sam noticed that every so often, Jitendhar would spill a few drops of his rice beer onto the floor. At first, Sam thought it was accidental, but when he saw it was deliberate, he asked Jitendhar why he was doing it.

"That is for *Maran Buru*, our creator," said Jitendhar. "When we talk of *bonga* or *dain*, we give *Maran Buru* some small offering to invite him into the conversation and for him to watch over us."

"I understand now," said Sam. "I have seen people do that before, but I just thought it was just incidental and part of the custom here. I didn't understand the significance of what was being done."

Having finished his *handi*, Jitendhar bid Sam good night as he went to his room for the night. Meanwhile, Sam was thinking about what he had learned. He had thought that he knew most of what went on in Begunkodar. Now he knew that though he had been here for more than a year, he had only begun to scratch the surface in his understanding of the Santal.

About a week later, Sam heard that a new stationmaster had arrived at Begunkodar Station. This was the railroad's response to Mohan's request to be transferred. Sam thought that he should get acquainted with the new man and develop a friendship with him so that his parcels would get proper treatment when they arrived. He didn't want one of his precious tins of coffee to go missing. Coffee could only be found for sale in the larger cities of India, and he didn't get to travel often away from the village.

Arriving at the station in midafternoon, Sam walked to the office of the stationmaster and knocked on the door. A rather tall man of light complexion opened the door and looked up and down at Sam, as though not understanding why someone looking like Sam might be standing there in front of him.

Speaking in Hindi, the stationmaster asked, "May I be of service to you, sir?"

Sam replied, also in Hindi, "Yes. I wish to introduce myself. I am Sam Edwards. I am here in Begunkodar bringing assistance to the village on behalf of the United States Peace Corps."

"Ah, so you must speak English, my American friend," said the man in excellent English. "My name is Rishabh. I am originally from New Delhi."

"It is good to meet you, Rishabh. I wanted to get acquainted with you, as I come to the station fairly often to pick up packages," said Sam, now speaking in English.

"It is good to meet you as well, Sam. I didn't know that any Americans were living in this part of West Bengal. How do you like the life here?"

"It is very different from where I grew up. But I find the people friendly, and they seem to like me. It is a different climate. The humidity is much higher here, but I am used to it now," Sam told him.

"Yes, it is warm and humid here most of the year," said Rishabh.

Sam was curious if Rishabh knew of the circumstances that had led to him being assigned to Begunkodar Station.

"Rishabh. How did you get assigned to this station?"

"I was looking for a new assignment in a part of the country I hadn't worked in before, and this one became available. I immediately took the opportunity. I arrived just yesterday and have met quite a few people here already. My assistant, who had been managing the station until I arrived, has been very helpful. But he seems a little quiet, and has not talked to me too much since I got here," said Rishabh.

Although Sam did not want to bring up the subject of Mohan's death, he spoke anyway.

"You must have heard about the last stationmaster here at Begunkodar?"

"Yes, Sam. A few people have mentioned that the last stationmaster here died under mysterious circumstances. They say that a spirit of a dead woman took his life from him."

"That's what they say," said Sam. "But I suspect that he just had a heart attack or stroke. He had been under a lot of stress since one of the villagers had been killed by an express train."

"I certainly can understand that," said Rishabh. "It must have been difficult for him to have someone die at the station under those circumstances."

Sam and Rishabh continued to talk, getting acquainted and sharing some of their lives with each other. After saying farewell to Rishabh, Sam rode on his motorbike back to the village, parked it at the house, and then went looking for Jitendhar. He found Jitendhar at a local eatery, drinking some tea and nibbling on black lentil bread.

"Jitendhar, I have some news for you," said Sam. "I have met the new stationmaster, and he seems like a nice and intelligent man. I think that he will become a welcomed member of the community."

"That is good to hear," said Jitendhar. "I wish him well in his new position as master of the station."

"So do I," said Sam.

Sam ordered some tea and bread for himself and sat with Jitendhar at his table. The two of them remained there until late afternoon and then walked together back to their house. After his evening meal with Jitendhar's family, Sam went to his room, washed up, and went to bed. He slept well that night.

The following day, Sam got up, shaved, dressed, and had his breakfast with the family. He had planned to talk to some of the village farmers today about planting new crops to sell at the local market. He wanted them to try growing different kinds of squash, as they were a good source of vitamins and nutrition. As he walked out towards the field where he was to meet with the farmers, he saw a few people talking rapidly, not too far away. They seemed a bit upset at something, as the conversation seemed serious and very animated. Sam thought it was probably just something gossipy about some people in the village.

Returning to his house for his afternoon meal, Jitendhar talked to Sam about what he heard had happened at the station the previous night.

"Sam," he said. "People here in the village are talking. The new stationmaster has said that last night, about four hours after the sun had gone down, he saw something out by the train tracks. He said that it looked like a woman in a white saree walking along the tracks. Then she disappeared in the darkness. Of course, everyone here in Begunkodar knows who that is. It is Noorie."

"Jitendhar, people say that Noorie's spirit took Mohan with her because he didn't try to help her when her saree got caught in the rail fastener. The new stationmaster was not here when Noorie was killed. He didn't have anything to do with her death. If this is true, why would her *bonga* still be at the station if her business there with Mohan is finished?" asked Sam.

"I don't know, Sam. Perhaps she is not yet finished with her business. Perhaps she wants something more."

"I don't know, Jitendhar. I don't think that this has anything to do with that poor woman Noorie. I think that when a person dies, they are gone forever. Nothing of them remains except the memory of them in those that still live."

Jitendhar smiled at Sam, then said:

"You may believe that, Sam, but the people here think in a different way. I understand that you have a different view, but we believe that the *bonga* of Noorie may stay here for three years or more before she completes her journey."

This was something that Sam had already learned. He knew that was the reason the cremated remains of Noorie were being kept at her family's house. This was to make sure that her spirit would be happy at the respect her family showed her in death through their performance of certain rituals. The bones would be fed ritually by female mourners in the family with milk, *handi*, and sacred water. This was part of the central Santal symbolism of flowers and bone in their culture. After the feeding of the bones, they would be crowned with flowers. This would show the connection of life and death through the flowers, which represented life through their fertility and women's fertility, and through ancestry, which the bones represented. Similar rituals would be carried out later. Eventually, after about three years, the spirit of the deceased, or *bonga*, would go to *hana puri*, the dwelling place of the dead.

The next day, Jitendhar told Sam that the newly arrived stationmaster had put in for a transfer. He had been there just barely three days, and already he wanted to leave.

Jitendhar told Sam that the reason for the stationmaster wanting to leave. Not only had he seen the *bonga* of Noorie again, walking along the railroad tracks, but a half dozen workers who were repairing a small section of tracks had also seen her. She had left some faint footprints where she had walked. The workers said that the footprints were pointed opposite from the direction Noorie had been walking, as though her feet were on backwards. They had told Rishabh what they had seen.

Sam was incredulous at hearing this. But he did not say anything to Jitendhar about his disbelief. He kept his thoughts to himself as he did not want to offend or belittle the beliefs of Jitendhar. He was sure that nothing would come from further expressions of his own thoughts, as the Santal people had believed and done things their way for millennia.

Sam decided that he would make another visit to the station late that afternoon. The stationmaster would be on duty then. He had to hear for himself what Rishabh had to say about his leaving. After all, he seemed such a reasonable and well-educated person.

About 4:30 that afternoon, Sam made the trip to the station. Arriving, he ran into Sripati, one of his neighbors who was about 38 years old. Sripati was a farmer and often shipped his rice on the railway. Sam spoke to him before he went into the station.

"Hello, Sripati," said Sam in Santali.

"Hello, neighbor. Why have you come to this accursed place, my friend?" said Sripati.

"I am here to speak with the stationmaster," Sam explained.

"Oh, yes. He will soon leave. I have heard this. He has seen the *bonga* and is now afraid of her. You go speak with him. Tell him to leave quickly before he is touched by her," urged Sripati.

Sam bid his neighbor goodbye and walked into the station. He went to the stationmaster's office, where he found Rishabh putting some of his things into a box.

Sam asked him, "Rishabh, why are you packing up to leave?"

"Hello, Sam. I am going to leave tomorrow. I have found that the story of the woman's spirit is true. I have seen her, and the track workers have seen her also. They told me that very same night I saw her. I am not going to take any chances with this situation. I know that the last stationmaster died under very strange circumstances, and I don't want to be another victim of this situation, even if this is something I can't fully understand. I have a family back in New Delhi, and I want to see them again. So, I have informed the railway that I am immediately quitting. If they want to hire me to work at a different location, that will be fine, but I am not going to stay here another night."

"I am sorry to see you going, Rishabh. We had just gotten acquainted, and you are leaving so soon," said Sam regretfully. He thought that he might have found a good friend in

Rishabh. Sam also felt comfortable talking with him, as though they had known each other for quite a while.

"I am sorry as well, Sam, but you can understand my feelings about this situation. I really can't stay any longer, even though it has just been three days. I hope that the poor woman's *aatma* or *bhaav* as we say in Hindi, her soul or spirit as you would say in English, finds peace."

"Rishabh, I wish you the best for your future life. I will miss you already. Take care," said Sam as he started walking out of the office.

"I wish you the best in your life also," said Rishabh.

Sam returned to the village and entered his house, where he found Jitendhar sitting and sipping some *handi*.

"Sam. What did the new stationmaster tell you about his leaving?" asked Jitendhar.

Sam explained that Rishabh said he was leaving immediately and that he believed he had seen Noorie's *bonga* and did not want to share the same fate as Mohan.

"It is the best for Rishaba to leave for his own sake," said Jitendhar. "I, too, am so sorry to hear the stationmaster was leaving after just starting his post."

Later that day, Sam saw the village *goret* passing from person to person, telling them that the *manjhi* had asked the village *ojha* to perform a special sacrifice at the *Jaher Garh* early the next morning. The gift was to try and appease the *bonga* of Noorie so that she would leave the station and not bother anyone again in the village. Sam's western skepticism was overcome by his curiosity, and he was looking forward to seeing the ceremony take place in the morning. He wondered what it would be like, and hoped it would give him a better understanding of the people he was living with. Although he had thought he knew and understood much of the Santal village culture, Sam now recognized he knew almost nothing of what was really important to the Santal.

Early the next morning, before anyone had eaten breakfast, the village men gathered at the *Jaher Garh* to watch and participate in the ritual sacrifice. The women and children were also there but stood outside of the inner circle of men. A steady rhythm was already pulsing from the *Tamak'* and *Tumdak'* drums, a regular part of the *saridhorom* or Santal religion. Sam arrived with his housemate Jitendhar, and asked him to explain what was taking place.

"Sam," said Jitendhar. "The *ojha* will place the young goat he is holding onto the ground. At that instant, his assistant will cut off the head of the goat in one stroke. Many of the men will rush in to get possession of the goat for good luck before it is to be burned in sacrifice."

When it was all done, Sam and Jitendhar returned to their house for their morning meal. Afterward, Sam went out in the fields to work with some of the village men on their projects. He returned home late in the afternoon. That evening, as Jitendhar and Sam were relaxing and drinking some *handi*, they talked of the sacrifice that was made that morning and how it would help the village.

"I believe that the *bonga* of Noorie will now be happy that the whole village has shown her respect," said Jitendhar.

"Do you think that there will be any more problems at the station?" asked Sam.

"I do not think so, my friend. I think that Noorie will now be satisfied,"

"I hope so," said Sam, still disbelieving in the presence of a spirit at the station. "I am just hoping that there will be someone at the station to receive any packages that have been sent to me."

"I am sure that you will still get your packages," said Jitendhar. "The station will stay open, and there are other station workers to keep your packages for you until you pick them up."

But Sam wasn't so sure. Many of the local workers had refused to go to the station after Mohan's death, and now that others believed they had seen the *bonga* of Noorie, almost no one was working at the station. Even the assistant stationmaster now refused to stay past late afternoon into the evening. They all believed that nighttime was the dominion of spirits, and wanted to be in the safety of their homes by nightfall.

More than a week passed, and there was no word of a new stationmaster being assigned at Begunkodar. Almost no one went to the station anymore to travel on the train. A person could purchase their ticket once aboard a train, but no one wanted to be around the station, even in the daylight.

Sam was concerned, as he was expecting one of the regular packages from his family. The small packages usually came about once every two or three weeks, and one was sure to arrive soon. He was hoping for some instant hot chocolate, which he had shared once before with his host family. The family seemed to enjoy it, and Sam's parents said they would try and send some to him again in the future. Sam was thinking about how he could make sure he got his package if no one was at the station to receive it.

Sam decided that he would go to the station in the early afternoon, before the train that usually brought his packages arrived. That way, he would receive the parcel in person. If it didn't arrive that day, he would see if he could make some arrangement with any person still working at the station and pay them to receive the package for him.

The next afternoon, he rode his motorbike to Begunkodar station and waited for the train he expected might have his package. When the train arrived to let off a couple of passengers, he spoke briefly to the freight handler on board. There was no package for him that day. However, the freight handler assured Sam that any package that arrived could be left with someone he authorized in writing. So, Sam looked for someone at the station to help him. There was no one in the ticket office or stationmaster's office, but Sam did find a freight handler nearby and made arrangements with him to receive any package that might come for Sam. Sam gave the freight handler a few rupees in advance and promised more when he got his package.

A few days later, Sam decided to return to the station. He had not been able to get away from his work until very late in the afternoon, and it was now rapidly approaching dark as he started on his motorbike. By the time he arrived at the station, the sun had set, and the light was fading quickly. Sam wandered outside the station for a few minutes, looking for the freight handler he had made arrangements with a few days earlier. Not finding him outside, he went into the station to look for him. It was dark inside. He could barely see the benches and seats inside the waiting room and didn't see anyone sitting there. There were no lights in the ticket office or elsewhere.

Sam stood for a few minutes in the waiting room as though expecting someone to show up. Nobody did, so Sam turned around and walked towards the door to the outside. He took a few steps but then hesitated as he thought he heard something. He listened but could only hear the sound of a few crickets.

Sam walked towards the door again and felt an icy chill on his skin. He smelled a slight hint of patchouli in the air. He stopped and then heard a very quiet giggle behind him. He turned slowly, and there, not more than three feet from him, stood the figure of a woman. She was almost invisible in the semi-dark, and she seemed almost transparent. She was dressed in a white saree. When Sam looked at her face, her skin was white, and her eyes were white orbs without color. Sam was not only startled but scared. He had never seen anything like her in his life and was ready to run out of the station. But he couldn't move his feet and somehow seemed so weak, as though his life energy was being drained from him.

Then, a soft and somehow faraway voice came to him. It seemed to be the phantom-like woman speaking, although her lips did not move and the sound came from all directions.

"Please, do not be afraid. I shall not harm you," the voice said in Santali. "I am Noorie, daughter of Jadab Kumari. I was once bound to this place, but am now free. You are a stranger among our people. I was curious about you, so that is why I am here now."

Sam was astounded. He realized that the Santal were right. *Bonga* did exist, and here he was, seeing and listening to one right in front of him. He tried to speak, although he was shivering and felt so weak.

"I am Sam," he managed to say in Santali. "I come from a far place. I am here to help your people."

"Thanks be to you, Sam. You are most welcome here. Peace be upon you and all of those that are with you," said Noorie.

"May you be happy and blessed," said Sam.

After Sam spoke to her, the specter of Noorie slowly faded away, and Sam was alone again in the waiting room. He found that he could move again but still seemed chilled to the bone. He slowly walked outside and welcomed the warm fresh air.

Sam walked to his motorbike, sat on the seat for a good half-hour, and then rode back to the village. He didn't speak to anyone of his experience, not even Jitendhar. A few days later, he heard that the station freight handler had received a package for him, and Sam made arrangements to get it from him. That arrangement worked out for the remaining eight months of his posting at Begunkodar.

Sam never went back to the train station again. When his posting ended, he gave his motorbike to Jitendhar and took a bus to Ranchi. From there, he made his way back to New Delhi. He was back in the United States after a couple of weeks.

Years later, thinking about his experiences in Begunkodar, Sam decided to check on what happened at the train station after he left. He found that the station had closed late in 1967. No one would use it anymore. People were still too afraid of encountering a *bonga*, or perhaps something even worse happening to them. Sam found that the train station remained closed until it reopened in 2009, but no one would work there after dusk. Few trains stopped there after dark. Everyone considered that station a haunted place, and the enigma of the spirit of Noorie remains an aspect in the lives of the people of Begunkodar.

The End

Halhogr Egod A.D.
by
Rajeev Bhargava

"Hey, Asvoria, come and look at this!" called Aegir. The middle-aged couple, both Norwegians, were in a dense forest, with hand luggage, backpacks, and spades, on a *holiday trip*. They were searching for artefacts belonging to Bigfoot. She made her way hurriedly towards him.

"What are you doing in that pit, Aegir?" she asked with a bemused look across her face. "Come out of there. This is no time for fun and games."

"Asvoria, this is not a prank, and please show some respect for our heritage. Don't forget, we are North Germanic."

"Yes, also known as Ascomanni, but instead of giving me this historical lecture, you still haven't explained why you are in that pit."

"It's *not a* pit. It's a giant foot belonging to Bigfoot!"

Asvoria rubbed her eyes and walked around it, rubbing her chin. "Hmm: you *might* just be right this time."

As if in reply, a thunderous roar sounded.

"Quick! Help me out of here before it comes back."

She knelt, reached out her arms, and carefully hauled him out of the footprint.

"How on *earth* did you fall inside in the first place?!" cried Asvoria, panicking.

"I didn't look where I was going. It just appeared, like a dip, and next thing I found myself sliding down." Once again, the roar sounded, and they decided to make a run for it in the opposite direction.

"Aegir, where are we going?"

"There's bound to be a bed and breakfast a couple of yards ahead for tourists. We'll stop there for the night, then continue our quest at dawn."

A short distance behind them, the stamping of heavy feet could be heard, heading in their direction, followed by yet another ferocious roar. They quickened their pace.

Suddenly, a tall and burly figure appeared before them. He waved his arms up and down as if signalling, or perhaps even warning them to stop. When they didn't, he blocked their path and stared down at them, infuriated.

"Stop!"

They froze in their tracks before him.

"Could he be…?" asked Asvoria to Aegir. Just then, the giant burst out in a fit of laughter.

"I am known by the name of Eotin, but you may call me Ettin."

"That's Anglo-Saxon!" quipped Aegir.

"Correct."

"Why, that's also an ogre's name, if I'm not mistaken," added Asvoria.

"Who are you? And why are you both here? Have you no fear of Bigfoot?"

"I am Aegir, and this lovely lady is my wife, Asvoria."

"Can't say I'm pleased to meet you. Now, as you are my guests, I ask you to accompany me to my abode. It's a short distance from here, through the forest and a stretch of river. Come; do not fear me."

Aegir glanced across at Asvoria nervously. She gave a shrug, and as they turned and followed Ettin, a large log landed just behind them.

"Halhogr Egod!" called out Ettin, and in a second, he lifted them both over his shoulders like rag dolls and lumbered forwards at full speed.

Sometime later, they arrived at a cottage. Ettin placed the couple carefully on the ground and wiped his forehead with his left forearm.

"Consider yourselves very lucky to be alive."

Just then, the cottage door opened, and a large female ogre emerged.

"Ettin! You have finally brought some guests with you, and after such a long time."

"Allow me to introduce my wife, Assay."

"We thank you for saving our lives and for your hospitality," said Asvoria, "but we can only spend the night here. Tomorrow, we need to continue on our quest to find and bring back evidence of Bigfoot."

Ettin gazed into her eyes, infuriated. "After all you've just been through? Why must you insist on finding evidence? Some things are best left … a mystery."

Assay ushered the couple to a table and seated them.

"Now wait here. Soup will be served shortly."

"Please make yourselves at home. I'm going out for a walk," said Ettin.

The moment he left, Aegir turned to Asvoria and whispered, "I can't help thinking we're being held here against our will."

"Don't be so paranoid, Aegir. We were both there at the scene. You saw what happened."

"Hmm; perhaps you're right. It's been a long and rough day. Let's try and get some sleep."

Outside, there was a full moon. Its glow fell across the cottage onto their faces.

****

The following day began with a chattering noise, accompanied by squeaks. Asvoria was the first to awaken, and she felt something sharp clamped on her neck.

"Eugeehh! Get off me! Someone, help me!" She had to use both her arms to pry it off.

The second bat was across Aegir's neck, and he appeared to be in a coma. No response.

Assay entered the room and hummed a lullaby, to which the bats responded and flew out the nearest window. She then opened a side cabinet drawer and brought out some antiseptic and a roll of bandages.

Panting for breath, Asvoria turned towards Aegir and shook him. No response. He flopped across the bed and fell on the floor.

"Oh no! Is he?..."

Assay knelt on the floor and felt his wrist. After she did so, her head bowed and she nodded.

"I … I'm so sorry, he is no more." She then attended to Asvoria with her medical kit.

"You planned all this, didn't you? Even the bats responded to your lullaby."

"You are wrong. I can assure you these bats are common visitors here. I tried all kinds of methods to lure them away, but they keep returning."

Just then, the door barged open and Ettin entered. "No sign of your Bigfoot!"

Asvoria broke down in tears. Assay shushed him and pointed to the floor where the bloody body of Aegir lay, his head slumped sideways.

"Oh no. I'm sure it was those bats again. Damn."

Asvoria wiped her eyes dry and looked around desperately. "I need a shovel."

"What for, dear?" queried Assay.

"To give my husband a decent burial … and after that, I'm leaving."

"But where will you go? What about your Bigfoot?"

"To hell with Bigfoot, or Halhogr Egod A.D., whatever you folk call him. My life is meaningless now."

"Is it *really*?" replied Ettin. "It was your husband's mission to take back with you some evidence. If you allow us, we can help provide that evidence. But first, we need to use Aegir's body as bait to lure Halhogr Egod here. Do you agree?"

Ettin turned towards Assay, gave a wry grin, and winked. He then produced a large syringe from his left side coat pocket and advanced towards Aegir.

"I will need to give you a dose of this first. Oh, do not be afraid. It's merely sedation to calm you."

"No, I won't take it. I think I'll leave now."

"But you cannot leave your beloved Aegir like that, for the bats, surely," said Assay. Their tone had changed now to a more menacing and intimidating one. They advanced closer and closer to Asvoria.

"No … no, keep away from me."

They both laughed hysterically at their helpless bait.

"Or else?" they called out simultaneously. The echoes of their laughter filled the air.

"One *final* warning to you both to keep away from me."

This time, both dashed towards her.

Suddenly, the ground beneath their feet shook until cracks appeared. Ettin and his wife Assay were taken by surprise, and the vibrations made them come crashing to the ground. To their shock, Asvoria metamorphosed; her body grew larger and larger. Hairs sprouted from everywhere until she was unrecognisable. The cottage smashed to the ground as she grew so large that even the treetops appeared like tiny plants around her.

"You puny, devious foolish people. Did you think for a moment that you could expose me to the world? All this time, it was *I* who was stalking *you!*"

Ettin and Assay turned to each other, taken aback, and tried to make a run to safety, but it was too late. Halhogr Egod knelt and clasped his right hand around them and lifted them to his lips with delicate precision. He licked his lips and devoured them in one swallow. He then looked into the forest and called out:

"Be warned, strangers. If *anyone* ventures out to expose my existence, then they will *all* share a similar fate. Some tales are best left untold."

The End

Faulty Products
by
Christopher Dabrowski

Krysia stared with disbelief at the mirror. *God, where are my eyelashes?* With shaking fingers, she touched the empty place.

There they are! I feel them! But why can't I see them? What is going on?

The mascara applied a few minutes ago effectively varnished them. Krysia used washing-up liquid which didn't bubble. It didn't work – she couldn't wash anything. What's more, it didn't pour on the sponge. How is it possible?

She found out about the efficacy of washing-up liquid an hour later during an attack of hemorrhagic fever. The washing-up liquid successfully cleansed her blood vessels of all dirt, including blood.

The End

A Stubborn Daughter by Matthew Wilson

I left her alone in the mines
Like a good father
I ignored her screams for days
Her pleas for a quick death.

The world is a harsh place
She would have to harden to survive
To learn my tricks
Many men have tried to kill me.

Stupidly she does not eat their bones
My little girl alone in the dark
Down there
It takes three days till she is near mad.

Finally, she listens to my wisdom
Changing her pale flesh to mist
She rises from that pit to my place
Worthy of a vampire's daughter to rule the night.

For a Lock of His Hair by Marge Simon

i.
I sold my dear soul
for a vampire's charms.
Now my handsome young Renfield
stays close by my side,
and young women envy me.

But for all the perks
that have come my way
still I'm not satisfied.
For a lock of his hair
I can have my soul back,
and with it, mortality.

This boyfriend of mine,
he's a simpleton, sure,
I've no use for him otherwise,
but a Demon Witch
wants his hair for a spell
that cannot be compromised.

ii.
I'm mortal again,
he's released from my thrall,
he's gone his way and I, mine.
I've lost my good looks,
I'm once more alone – Oh no!
Can it be that I miss him?

Revenge for dead friends by Matthew Wilson

Firing volleys at the body
Tied to a hangman's tree
Howling a last ignored wish
The sedative of silver bullets.

The Driven
by
Denny E. Marshall

A crowd is chasing them.

Sue, Beth, and Matt run to Beth's truck and speed off. Behind them, four cars are in pursuit. Soon the three are boxed in. They depart the vehicle and run into an abandoned factory.

It's hasn't been the same since zombies learned to drive.

The End

About the Contributors

Linda Barrett:

    Ms. Barrett has been writing all her life. She wrote her first book at the age of eight. It's still in the McKinley Elementary school library. She was published in the *Huntingdon Junior Library* literary magazine by age thirteen. She's won three awards with the Montgomery County Community College Writer's contest. "Mr. Cat's Revenge" won third place in the 2014 MCCC contest. Ms. Barrett lives with her 84 years young mother in Abington in the same house for 50 years."

Rajeev Bhargava:

    Rajeev lives in Harrow with his parents and five Chihuahuas. He has been writing since the age of twelve but had his first work published in 1990. Since then he's been writing stories, poems and articles for the small press as well as mainstream. His ambition is to be a freelance writer.

Margaret L. Carter:

    Reading *Dracula* at the age of twelve ignited Margaret L. Carter's interest in a wide range of speculative fiction and inspired her to become a writer. Vampires, however, have always remained close to her heart. Her work on vampirism in literature includes *Dracula: The Vampire and the Critics, The Vampire in Literature, A Critical Bibliography,* and *Different Blood: The Vampire as Alien.* She holds a PhD in English from the University of California (Irvine), and her dissertation contained a chapter on *Dracula.* In fiction, she has written horror, fantasy, and paranormal romance. Recent publications include *Crimson Dreams* (vampire romance), *Demon's Fall* (paranormal romance novella), *Heart's Desires and Dark Embraces* (story collection, fantasy and paranormal romance), and *Legacy of Magic* (sword and sorcery, in collaboration with her husband, Leslie Roy Carter). Her short stories have been published in anthologies such as the "Sword and Sorceress" and "Darkover" volumes, among others. "A Walk in the Mountains," co-written with her husband, appeared in the 2016 anthology *Realms of Darkover.* A sequel, "Believing," was included in *Masques of Darkover* (2017). Margaret's solo humorous ghost story, "Haunted Book Nook," appeared in the anthology *Sword and Sorceress* 33 (2018). She and her husband, a retired naval officer, live in Maryland and have four sons, several grandchildren and great-grandchildren, a St. Bernard, and two cats.

Christopher T. Dabrowski:

    Christopher has had numerous books published in the USA and Poland. His USA works include: *Anomaly* and *Escape*, both published by the Royal Hawaiian Press. Books published in Poland include *Anima Vilis* (Initium), *Grobbing* (Novae Res), *Deathbirth and other Stories* (Agharta & Amoryka), *Orgazmokalipsa* (Alternatywne publishing house), *Anomalia* (Forma publishing house), and *Ucieczka* (2017 - Dom Horroru publishing house). Monika Olasek provided the English translation for his *Night to Dawn* stories.

Sandy DeLuca:

    Sandy has written five novels; *Settling in Nazareth* (she painted the cover art), *Descent, Manhattan Grimoire, From Ashes,* and *Requiem for the Dead.* Her poetry chapbook, *Burial Plot in Sagittarius* (also created cover art and illustrations), was nominated for the BRAM STOKER award in 2001. Her art has been exhibited in galleries, hair salons, book stores and online venues. She has also painted covers and contributed interior illustrations for various numerous small press venues.

Jon M. Fox:

    Jon M. Fox is a writer of experimental fiction, non-fiction and poetry. A former educator, Jon's writing has appeared in such diverse publications as *An Indigenous Message on Obscure Archaeological Literature.* Jon's fictional writing and poetry frequently focuses on the genre of magical realism, largely stemming from his Yaqui indigenous heritage and life experiences. When he isn't reading or writing, he's busy with various projects in Jaen, Nueva Ecija Province in the Philippines, where he spends his time, when not in the United States, engaged in community economic development, and sharing his time with his wife and family.

Chris Friend:

  Chris has published his art in small press horror magazines for nearly 25 years. His surreal horror images have been featured in *Stygian Articles, Realm of the Vampire, Deathrealm, Black Petals,* and *Space and Time.* He draws his inspiration from Harry Clarke, H. R. Giger, and the horror comics of the 70s such as the Tomb of Dracula her and the Hammer Studios Frankenstein films. Chris friend can be reached at Mars_art_13@yahoo.com. Chris Friend can be reached at Mars_art_13@yahoo.com.

  To sample his illustrations, go to http://chris.michaelherring.net and http://www.moonlit-path.com/art-2-13-06.htm.

Todd Hanks:

  The creative writing of Todd Hanks has been seen in publications such as *Asimov's Science Fiction* Magazine and the *Kansas City Star* newspaper.

Tom Johnson (7/26/1940 – 11/04/2019:

  Tom was a Vietnam veteran, having done 20+ years in the US Military as a Military Policeman, then turned his talents to writing. He enjoyed literary success as a science fiction novelist with his action adventures in the Jurassic Period of Earth's predawn. His *Jur* series novels were quite successful. He has created short story SF characters like Captain Danger of the Space Rangers and the galactic master thief, The Forever Man, as futuristic space opera adventures. His many costumed crime fighters include two of his own creations, such as The Black Ghost and The Masked Avenger, as well as a western masked hero called The Nightwind.

Hal Kempka:

  Hal's stories have been published in numerous magazines and ezines including *Night to Dawn, Blood Moon Rising, Black Petals, Inner Sins, Sanitarium, Yellow Mama,* and *Microhorror.* His horror short fiction anthologies, *Blue Plate Special* and *Discarded Treasures,* are currently available on Amazon Kindle, Barnes and Noble, and Smashwords, among others. *Discarded Treasures* is available in both paperback and e-book. Other anthologies including his stories are Pill Hill Press: *Zombie Art Inspired Short Stories, Blood Bound Books: Seasons in the Abyss,* and Post Mortem Press: *Shadowplay.*

Hillary Lyon:

  With an MA in English Literature from SMU, Hillary Lyon founded and for 20 years served as senior editor for the independent poetry publisher, Subsynchronous Press. Her speculative, horror, and sci-fi stories have appeared in numerous print and online publications. She's also an illustrator for horror/sci-fi, and pulp fiction sites. And she loves to hand-paint furniture and accessories.

Rod Marsden:

  Rod Marsden hails from Sydney, Australia. He has three degrees related to writing and history. His stories have been published in Australia, England, Russia, the USA and now Canada. He has work in the American anthology *Cats Do it Better,* the American steam punkanthology *Break Time* and in the Canadiananthology *Morbid Metamorphosis.* Many of his short stories have been published in *Night to Dawn* magazine. His books include *Undead Reb Down Under and Other Vampire Stories, Disco Evil: Dead Man's Stand, Ghost Dance,* and *Desk Job* (his salute to Lewis Carroll). *Cold Water Conscience* is his venture into Crime/Horror. His short play, *Zombie Vision,* was well received at Cronulla Arts Theatre. His play *Hyde and Seek* was even better received. Rod has a fondness for Cronulla and the Wollongong area but an abiding love for the more northern Clarence River region of his home state of New South Wales.

Denny E. Marshall:

  Denny E. Marshall has had art, poetry, and fiction published. Some recent credits include interior art in *Midnight Echo #14* Dec. 2019, cover art for *Society Of Misfit Stories* Feb. 2020, and poetry in *Space & Time Magazine #134* Fall 2019. This year his website is celebrating 20 years on the web. Also in 2020 his artwork is for sale for the first time. It is available on Zazzle as posters coffee cups, puzzles, mouse pads, etc. The link is on his website. (Click on top left drawing.) See more at www.dennymarshall.com.

Elizabeth Hattie Pierce-Collins:

Elizabeth first learned art and drawing from her mother. From there, she was self-taught until she was able to attend art school. She loves drawing the human figure and never stops studying the human body in motion. Her illustrations have appeared in *Night to Dawn* magazine and *The Spider's Web* (a novel). These have drawn positive attention from the readers. Elizabeth hopes to appear in more magazines and books in the future. For more information, contact Elizabeth at wackyursalinan45@aol.com.

Marc Shapiro:

Marc has been a busy beaver. His story *Let Me Take You Down* was printed in book form in the Short Sharp Shocks imprint of Demain Publishing on December 31. Upcoming from Demain is his debut poetry collection *Existential Jibber Jabber*. Already out: his unauthorized biography of Keanu Reeves entitled *Keanu Reeves Excellent Adventure* (Riverdale Avenue Books) and the shortest story he's ever written, four sentences under 100 words, on the website Warp 10 Lit. Marc Shapiro has a very patient and understanding wife.

Marge Simon:

Marge Simon's works appear in publications such as DailySF Magazine, Pedestal, Dreams& Nightmares. She edits a column for the HWA Newsletter, "Blood & Spades: Poets of the Dark Side," and serves as Chair of the Board of Trustees. She won the Strange Horizons Readers Choice Award, 2010, and the SFPA's Dwarf Stars Award, 2012. She has won three Bram Stoker Awards ® for Superior Work in Poetry, two first place Rhysling Awards and the Grand Master Award from the SF Poetry Association, 2015. In addition to her poetry, she has published two prose collections: *Christina's World*, Sam's Dot Publications, 2008 and *Like Birds in the Rain*, Sam's Dot, 2007. Her poems appear in *Qualia Nous* (Written Backwards), *The Dark Phantastique* (Jasunni Productions), Spectral Realms anthologies by S.T. Joshi, and more poems will appear in *Chiral Mad 3* and *Scary Out There*, a HWA/ Simon & Schuster Y/A collection, 2015. www.margesimon.com

Matthew Wilson:

Matthew Wilson has had over 150 appearances in such places as *Horror Zine, Star*Line, Spellbound, Illumen, Apokrupha Press, Gaslight Press, Sorcerers Signal* and many more. He is currently editing his first novel and can be contacted on twitter @matthew94544267.

Lee Clark Zumpe:

Lee Clark Zumpe has been writing and publishing horror, dark fantasy and speculative fiction since the late 1990s. His short stories and poetry have appeared in a variety of publications such as *Weird Tales, Space and Time* and *Dark Wisdom;* and in anthologies such as *Dark Horizons, Best New Zombie Tales Vol. 3, Dread Shadows in Paradise, Heroes of Red Hook* and *World War Cthulhu*. His work has earned several honorable mentions in *The Year's Best Fantasy and Horror* collections.

An entertainment columnist with Tampa Bay Newspapers, Lee has penned hundreds of film, theater and book reviews and has interviewed novelists as well as music industry icons such as Paddy Moloney of The Chieftains and Alan Parsons. His work for TBN has been recognized repeatedly by the Florida Press Association, including a first-place award for criticism in the 2013 Better Weekly Newspaper Contest.

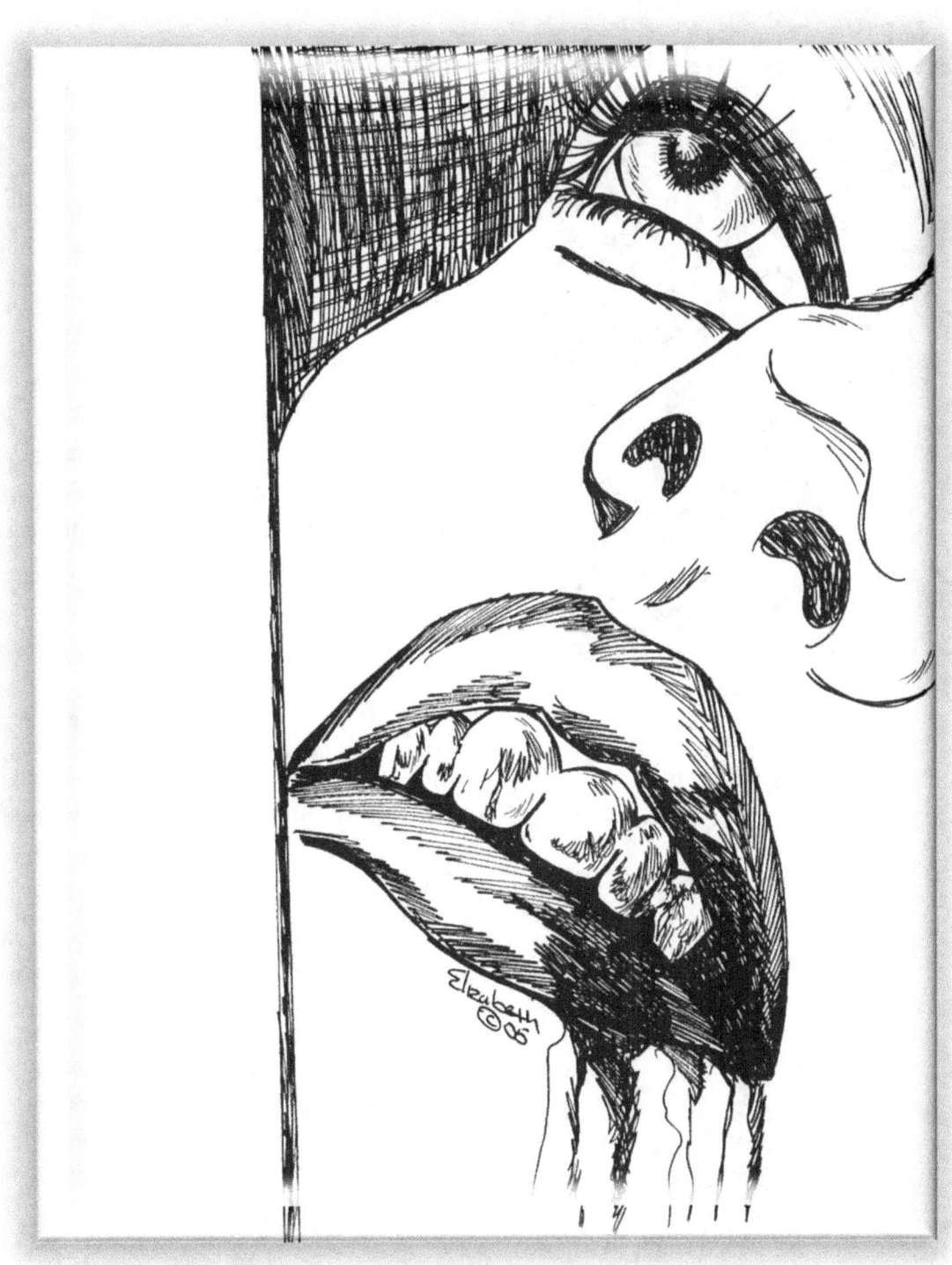

He's seventeen, the world is dying around him, while half the country lies between him and his surviving family. He has a good dog, a child, a dying farmer, and decent ranchers to help him – against him are vicious bikers, the greedy, the foolish and the evil. But Jason is learning every step of the way.

Available at:

Amazon
Barnes & Noble
Book Depository and other retailers
Lyn McConchie | NIGHT TO DAWN MAGAZINE & BOOKS Lyn McConchie (bloodredshadow.com)

At the age of forty, psychiatrist Roger Darvell discovered vampires are real, a nonhuman species living secretly among the ordinary mortals who vastly outnumber them, and he himself is a hybrid, with a vampire mother and a human father. After learning the truth about the craving for blood that had plagued him all his adult life, he came to terms with his "monstrous" side and found love with his human professional partner, Dr. Britt Loren. In between treating their mundane patients, Roger and Britt occasionally venture into problems of the paranormal. They deal with three extraordinary cases in these stories, as they counsel a neurotic young vampire, a guilt-ridden werewolf, and a woman who owns a haunted antique desk. Available at:

Amazon
Barnes & Noble
Margaret L. Carter Margaret L. Carter (bloodredshadow.com)

www.ingramcontent.com/pod-product-compliance
Lightning Source LLC
Chambersburg PA
CBHW080753120626
46557CB00005B/1249